Crimson Hearts

Nicole Reeves

Published by Nicole Reeves

Printed in the United States of America

First U.S. Edition: October 2020

ISBN: 978-1-7357037-0-1 (paperback)

ISBN: 978-1-7357037-1-8 (ebook)

Library of Congress Control Number: 2020917976

Author: Nicole Reeves

Editor: Melissa Frey

Cover Design: Naomi Gibson

For my daughter, Kinley.
I will forever see you in butterflies, in rainbows,
and as the brightest star in the night sky.
Until we meet again,
Mommy loves you.

1

Party like a Wallflower

COLLEGE PARTIES ARE NOT my idea of a well-spent Saturday night.

This particular one has a dress code that no one bothered to inform me about. Every girl here is wearing denim shorts that might as well be underwear and crop tops that look painted on, so I look pretty strange in my plain white t-shirt and black leggings.

I'm glad I opted for the fancier of the two pairs of shoes in my suitcase. I'd left my signature Converse in the hotel and donned a borrowed pair of black stiletto heels for the night. I'm not excellent at walking in them, but when you're a wallflower, you don't do much walking anyway. I'll have to thank my best friend, Sam, for tossing them in there. At least I kind of look like I tried.

To be fair, the temperature is probably still in the nineties outside, despite being almost ten PM. The sun has been down for a few hours, but the Saturday evening air still feels hot and sticky. Late August in Texas can be a real killer.

I can feel a couple of scantily-clad girls eyeing me from across the room, and I wish I could see Danny's head poking up above the crowd like usual. The problem is, this fraternity is full of tall, muscular jocks, and he blends right in.

The music is thumping loudly through large speakers in the shared living area of the house, and I feel as if my teeth might vibrate out of my skull. The walls are painted maroon and white, Texas A&M school colors, and at least a dozen class photos cover them in perfectly-matching frames. The wood floors stick to my heels with every step, and the entire house smells like spilled beer and musty cologne. I wish someone would open a window. It's not a pleasant smell.

I still don't know how I let Danny talk me into coming to this party with him. He's the social one—I'm just the tagalong twin. He knew what he was doing earlier when he bribed me with a trip to the George H.W. Bush Presidential Library and Museum. My little nerd heart rejoiced before we even set foot inside—I probably would have agreed to a root canal in exchange for that tour.

Danny is being scouted by the Texas A&M football program. I am interested in the school as well, but for completely different reasons. Namely, that my brother is interested, and I want to be wherever he is. I don't know how to exist anywhere that he's not—he's my home. And since we only have one year left of high school, this is decision-making time.

"You look like you need a drink." A pretty blonde girl smiles at me while balancing two red solo cups in her palms. She extends one to me. "It's just Sprite. I didn't take you for the alcohol-drinking type. I'm Andi."

I smile back at her and take the cup from her hand—it does smell like Sprite. "Thanks, I'm Henrietta..." I shake my head, quickly catching the mistake. "Hattie, it's just Hattie." Only Dad calls me Henrietta.

I tuck my long hair behind my ear, a nervous habit. Andi is wearing those cut-off jean shorts where the pockets hang lower than the hem and a maroon crop top that says "Go Aggies" across the chest. She looks like she fits right in around here.

"Where are you from, doll?" she says, her southern accent clearly not from Texas.

I doubt she's heard of our tiny town. "McKinley Lake. It's a little town in the middle of nowhere. We're about an hour from Waco, though—you know, the home of all things shiplap? Chip and Joanna land."

Andi squeals. "Oh, girl, I just love her style! I'm from 'bama, born and raised. Texas is the furthest I've been from home, but I like it here. People are so friendly!"

I'm not from Texas either, but I don't feel the need to tell this perfect stranger my whole life story. I save that for people like my brother who I've known for more than a minute. Speaking of which, where the heck is he?

"College tour weekends are my favorite. And just so you know, these parties are a lot more chill than the school-year ones, because not everyone is back from summer break just yet." She laughs. "Are y'all hoping to come here?"

I bite my lip and look around for Danny one last time. Social situations are my least favorite—I always let Danny do the talking for both of us.

"My brother is being scouted for the football team. I'm just moral support." It's not a lie, but it's not the whole truth, either. I am hoping to come here for my own reasons, too. The military history of this school comforts me—the army runs in my blood. Though I want to get an English degree, which luckily I can do from just about anywhere, I'm pretty positive that, with my grades, I can follow Danny wherever he ends up going.

"Go Aggies!" Andi pumps a fist in the air. "We have an excellent athletics program! I'm here on a Track and Field scholarship."

"Then you and my brother would definitely get along. Unfortunately, I do not enjoy physical activity. If I'm running, the world is probably ending."

"Ha—you're funny!" She looks down toward the floor. "I love your shoes, by the way. With legs like that, I was sure you were an athlete."

I shake my head. I have been forced into regular exercise my whole life. Dad has always stressed the importance of being battle ready even though we're not in the army ourselves. He believes in fit bodies and sharp minds. Running three miles five times a week for the last twelve years has been nothing short of torture. "Never by choice," I say. "I'd rather work out my brain than my body."

"Fair enough—college is a good place for that, too. I wish I cared more about that part. Though there are a lot of super-cute guys around here, too, if you're interested in more than just books." She stares at someone behind me. "Don't panic, but there's one headed our way right now."

I feel his weight drop down on my shoulders from behind as he wraps his arms around my neck. "Hatts, you makin' friends?" He laughs in my ear, and I feel myself relaxing. Danny smells like he's had a little more to drink than soda—Dad will just love that when we get back to the hotel.

I straighten my spine, trying not to buckle under his weight. "This is Andi. We were just talking about you and the football team." I'm thankful he's here. This girl is pretty, and I know Danny will gladly take over the conversation. "Andi, this is my brother, Dan..."

"Daniel Tate," Danny interrupts me, taking Andi's hand and shaking it gently.

"Daniel?" I whisper, eyebrows raised.

"It sounds more mature." He winks at me.

"You, mature? Now that's hilarious."

"Nice to meet ya, Daniel. Y'all are gonna love being Aggies if you come here." Andi grins at my brother, the typical reaction to his good looks. I try to take it as a compliment, since we look so much alike. Boy-girl twins cannot be identical, of course, but no one will ever doubt that we're from the same gene pool.

Other than our drastic height difference, it's obvious we're related. Dad was generous with his genes. We inherited the Tate-signature bright-green eyes, dark hair, tanned skin, and athletic build, so we can't really complain. We didn't get much from our mother, but that was true in every area of our lives.

Danny and Andi lapse into a comfortable conversation, and I let my mind wander. I sip my Sprite slowly, watching the crowd. Most people are dancing together or pressed into every possible sitting area, engaging in animated conversations. I feel a little jealous when I see how comfortable and easy it looks for everyone else. It's not that I don't like people—I do. I just get nervous and quiet around new people.

I've always been shy and slow to open up—just ask Sam. Even though we met in the fifth grade and were both fairly new to the area, it took me awhile to fully open up to her. Now we are thick as thieves, and I'm so glad she stuck with me despite my quirks.

But I'd rather stay in and read a book or watch TV shows and live vicariously through the characters on the page or the screen. Life's less messy that way.

Especially because I have a black belt in embarrassing myself. Danny is ten inches taller than my vertically challenged height of five foot two, and I think all of my outgoing personality must have been stored in those missing inches. That, or he stole it all in the womb.

"Hattie, did you hear me?" Danny is laughing at something, and he and Andi are both looking at me like they're waiting for me to say something. Typical Hattie: I zoned out, and now I look like a jerk.

"Sorry? I was watching those people dance." I shrug.

"Ooh, yes! Let's all dance!" Andi squeals, grabs my hand, and drags me toward the mass of people gyrating against each other. I look back at Danny for help, my eyes pleading, but he just smirks. I'm not getting any help from him, but as Andi yanks me along, I can't worry about that now. I'm using all my concentration not to snap an ankle in these heels or spill my drink on someone.

"Yeah, Hattie, let's all dance." He winks, following closely behind.

"I am going to kill you later." I mouth the words to him.

"Aww, love you, too, punk." He ruffles my hair and falls in behind Andi.

This night just went from uncomfortable to nightmarish. I will definitely make him pay later.

———— ♡ ♡ ♡ ————

We had a 0500 wake up because Sergeant Dad was less than impressed with Danny's drinking last night and this morning's apparent hangover. I had to half-carry my drunk brother last night from our Uber to the hotel room, the smell of beer on him assaulting my senses, impossible to miss. We made it to the room just in time for our midnight curfew at least, but Danny clearly wasn't going to major in any drinking sports.

In a rare turn of events, I am the clear winner of the "favorite child" games this morning. It's 0630 now, and I'm sitting in the front seat of our SUV next to Dad, the last book from my summer reading list for AP English in my lap.

School starts on Monday, and I am nothing if not academically prepared. I have to be—Mr. Galloway is a tough teacher. I think he made the reading list extra-challenging on purpose, clearly trying to weed out the weak. But he won't break me. I'm not trying to go Ivy League or anything, but I do want to get a full-ride academic scholarship if I can swing it. Though he doesn't expect it, I'd feel better about not leaving Dad with a huge financial burden.

"Stop reading in the car, Hattie—it's making me sick," Danny moans from the back seat. He's sprawled across the leather seat, a pillow propped under his head, his brown hair sticking up all over the place. The leather seats are air-conditioned, so he's not suffering that badly.

"Some of us want to be prepared for school," I snap back a little too loudly. "And how are you getting sick? You can't even see my book from where you are."

"But I know you're reading, and it makes me want to puke. Can't you give it a rest?" He throws a half-empty water bottle over the seat, and I hear the swish of the water just as it hits me in the head.

"Consider it payback for the dancing." I am about to launch the bottle directly at Danny's gut when I catch Dad giving me a hard look. He reaches out and takes the bottle from me, tucking it into his door pocket.

"Maybe you wouldn't feel so sick if you hadn't made poor choices last night," he says, shifting his eyes back to the road. He's unusually calm this morning, and if he wasn't driving us home, I'm willing to bet Danny would be getting a lot more than the cold shoulder. When it comes to rules and discipline, Sergeant Dad doesn't mess around.

I drop back against my seat and stare out the window at the flat Texas landscape. The car goes quiet—it's never fun when Dad gets annoyed. We will likely pay for this drama in chores when we get home.

"Sergeant Dad" isn't just a nickname or a funny joke. My dad is Retired Command Sergeant Major Tate of the U.S. Army. Yeah, it's a mouthful. He spent over twenty years serving in combat and commanding men and women in extreme conditions. Now that he's retired, he forgets that life at home isn't a battlefield. We aren't his soldiers—we are his children. Unfortunately for us, Dad doesn't really see a difference between the two.

He retired six years ago, but we didn't exactly leave the military life behind. We moved from Fort Drum in Upstate New York to McKinley Lake, a speck of a town in Texas. It's only an hour from Waco, but it's hours away from any real entertainment. It's actually not very far away from Fort Hood, which happens to be one of the largest army bases in the world—which is why Dad chose it. He runs his own private contracting company, sending soldiers-turned-civilians overseas under government contracts. He recruits them as they leave the military so they have a smooth transition to civilian life and are able to make a lot more money working the same jobs they did in the army.

I almost wish we'd just moved to Killeen, a small town outside of Fort Hood. No one moves there for the fun of it, but at least the kids there are mostly army brats, so making friends would have been a lot simpler. None of the kids at our school understand our army upbringing.

"Anyone hungry?" Dad asks, pulling me from my thoughts.

"I could eat." I can always eat. "Danny, you might feel better if you eat something."

Danny groans again. "I'm an idiot. I feel like hot garbage. I'll try anything."

"I'll stop at the next exit," Dad says. "I saw a sign for a local breakfast joint. They should have eggs; they're good for your condition. But what I *should* do is make you run it off."

I chime in. "Dad, running isn't exactly a punishment to him. He'd probably enjoy it. He and Kellan ran ten miles on Friday to make up for him missing practice this weekend." Football is Danny's religion, and working out is how he worships his deity. Kellan is Danny's best friend, and he also drinks the football Kool-Aid. The entire town partakes of this madness.

Danny huffs at my comment. "We have a game next Friday, and McKinley Lake High is not going to take this season lying down. I have a legacy to build."

"Whoo-freaking-hoo, go Crimson Wolves," I say with zero enthusiasm, my fist in the air.

Dad snickers. "Hattie, would it kill you to have just a little school spirit? Danny and Kellan have been working diligently on new plays and team morale this summer. The whole town thinks they have a shot at the division title this year with your brother leading them. He's building community—you could learn something from him."

I can almost feel the heat from the invisible fire Danny's eyes are sending my way. "I don't need community; I have my brain, and I have Sam." I pull down my visor mirror and run my middle finger over my lips to smear in my lip balm. I'm not sure if Danny sees the gesture I intended for him, but when Dad frowns, I know that *he* has. My favorite-child badge has clearly been revoked.

Danny and I talk a lot of smack to each other, and we're constantly giving each other crap. But we don't really mean it. He's the most important person in my life—our twin bond is strong.

Dad takes the exit for Granny's Place, a cute little restaurant on the side of the interstate made to look like a log cabin. We pull into a parking spot, and Dad turns off the car but doesn't make a move to get out.

Dad's scarred and weathered hands grip the wheel as he takes a deep breath. He has his sergeant face on, so I brace myself. "I know you two are about to be seniors this year, but I want to be clear. You are still part of the Tate family, and, as such, I expect you to hold yourself to a higher standard. Have some decorum. While I'm not particularly impressed with you drinking last night, I appreciate that the two of you stayed together and made it home safely." He sighs. "Your birthday is only two months away, and then, in the eyes of the law, you will be adults. I don't necessarily believe that at some magical age you become an adult, however. I believe that the title is earned. Please make me proud."

"Yes, Sir," we echo. We have been well trained.

"Excellent. Let's go get some chow," Dad says, and I am not about to argue with that.

2

Headaches and Hangovers

WE PULL ONTO OUR street just after ten AM. The Texas A&M campus is only a three-hour drive from home, which also adds to its appeal. Though I'm not super close with Dad, he is our only real family.

I look up at the two-story white house with black shutters which screams Southern charm. The house is probably my favorite thing about moving here—it's huge. It's clean and tidy, and the lawn is lush, green, and manicured to perfection year-round.

I adore the old trees that pepper the lawn and give it character. They also provide just enough shade for me to lie underneath them and look up at the expanse of pale blue. I miss the wilderness of New York, but there's something to be said about the Texas sky.

I spy Sam's red car parked on the far end of the three-car garage as we approach the house. Dad has assigned her a specific spot—he really likes things orderly. "Looks like your girlfriend is here," Danny calls out as we bump into the driveway. I'm not surprised; I sent her a text when we were thirty minutes out.

"May I go to the lake with Sam for a few hours, Dad? I promise I'll finish my notes for English while I'm there." I'm hoping he'll take pity on me—today's the last day of summer vacation. I put my swimsuit on under my jean shorts and NASA shirt this morning in anticipation.

Dad pulls up next to Sam's car and kills the engine. He turns around to face Danny. "Are you going to survive now that you've eaten something? Maybe you want to join the girls at the lake?"

I hear Danny snort. "I think I'll just go see what Kellan is up to, but thanks for the offer."

I think about telling him I didn't offer, but I don't want to upset Dad. He doesn't always appreciate or understand our friendly banter. "Thanks, Dad!" I yell, rushing out before he can say anything else. I grab my bag from the trunk and toss it at Sam.

"Geez! You need all this crap for the lake?" Sam laughs, her strawberry-blonde ponytail swinging as she pops her trunk and drops my bag inside. She's wearing her favorite red one-piece swimsuit and a white-lace beach cover-up. Her flip-flops are a matching red. The girl has style, and she'll tell you as much.

"I stuffed it full of snacks from the hotel." I shrug.

She curtseys. "My hero."

"Do you have an extra pair of sandals in that heap of yours?"

"Well, do one-legged ducks swim in circles?" Her eyebrows wiggle.

I stop and look at her. "Do they?"

"Who knows? Roll with it." Sam opens her car door and climbs in. She pulls down her sun visor and opens up a lip gloss. "Get in already. Summer is almost over!"

The lake is mostly deserted when we arrive. The sandy strip holds a handful of families on picnic blankets, but the dock is deserted. Everyone is probably getting ready for the big first day of school tomorrow. I've been ready for weeks—I don't do well without a schedule and things to keep my mind busy. Sam doesn't feel quite the same way about summer ending, though.

I slip on the pair of black sparkly flip-flops Sam hands me, leaving my Converse safely behind in her car. I don't want them to get all sandy before school tomorrow.

We carry our towels down to the short pier and find a good spot.

McKinley Lake isn't very big, but it's clear and deep enough to dive off the dock when we get too hot. It used to be bigger back when they named the town, and it still floods higher sometimes, but it seems to get a little smaller each year. Luckily, our population is small, so it does the job. It's not bad to look at, either; the Texas sky disappears at the water's edge.

"Where the heck are Danny and Kellan?" Sam asks me while I help her apply sunscreen on her back. With her fair skin, she needs a lot more protection than I do.

"Probably doing something sweaty and boring."

"Sweaty and those bods? How can that be boring for you? They're like extras from that *Gladiator* movie. Golden. Freaking. Gods. Those rippling muscles on Danny..." She fans herself.

"Samantha Marie Ellis, please don't make me gag. That is my brother you're drooling over." I stick my finger down my throat in a mock gag.

Sam rolls her eyes. "Listen, you're his twin, and you're hot as hell. So don't pretend you don't know what a fine specimen your brother is. The entire population of McKinley High cannot be wrong."

"We have an agreement, Sam," I remind her.

"Yeah, yeah. I can't date him because I'm your best friend, and it would be weird. I still hold out that you might change your mind someday. Take mercy on your bestie." She sighs dramatically.

I try not to laugh. I know she's not wrong about him being attractive, but it's just gross to think about Danny like that. Years ago, I made her swear she wouldn't go after Danny. If they broke up and I had to pick a side, that would be absolute hell. Kellan, on the other hand, I have been known to drool over, but the same rule applies. Best friends are off-limits.

Kellan and Danny have been best friends for as long as Sam and I have. They'd bonded over their mutual love of sports immediately. When we first moved to town, a bunch of boys on the local sports teams had been less than thrilled—Danny excels at every physical activity he tries, which intimidates people. They didn't want some outsider coming in and snatching up their spots in the lineup.

Kellan had been the one to turn them around. He liked Danny, so he stuck his neck out for him. Told the kids they should embrace the fact that they might actually start winning some games with his help. And just like that, Danny was in—and the bromance was strong.

That's just how Kellan is; he's a sweet soul. He loves football but not the way Danny does. Kellan likes the way it brings people together, the way it forges brotherhood and friendship. He likes the traditions and people.

I love knowing that about him. Sharing a Jack and Jill bedroom with your brother comes in handy—you can hide in the tub and listen in on juicy conversations when he has someone over. Not that I've done that... I just know a lot more about Kellan than I care to admit. Like the fact that he knows the words to all of the Jonas Brothers' songs, cries during romcoms, and will kill Danny with his bare hands if he ever tells anyone that.

"You think any more about what you want to do when we graduate?" I ask Sam, hoping to lead the conversation to a more neutral territory.

She sees right through me and glares before flopping onto her stomach. "Yeah, I am going to apply for a couple of schools with music programs. Even if I just end up teaching choir somewhere, I'd be okay with that."

Angelic doesn't even come close to describing Sam's voice. She could give Adele a run for her money with her range. She still wants to try out for The Voice or America's Got Talent, but her mom and dad would prefer she go to school either way.

"Remember when you forced me to try out for the school musical with you?" I snicker at the memory.

"You could have warned me that it sounds like someone is being murdered when you sing." Sam slaps at me.

"I *told* you I couldn't sing. I *told* you I'd just die of embarrassment up there." It felt like I had.

"You're still here, so... don't be so dramatic. Plus, you made me sound even better, so it was still worth it." She grins.

"You're incorrigible."

Sam groans. "Don't use words like that with me, Hattie—this isn't the SATs."

"I like to use big words—why bother being an English major otherwise?"

"Uh... there is no good reason to do that to yourself. *Bo-ring*," she singsongs back.

Clearly, Sam does not share my love of the written word. "Oh well—you won't be saying it's boring when I'm writing for your favorite TV show someday."

"Touché."

Sam and I are always like this. Banter and love for days. She's the wild, carefree one, and I'm the shy, reserved one. She talks me into doing things I would never do otherwise, and I rein her crazy ass in. We balance each other out.

I hit the best friend jackpot when she chose me. That first day she came to town, fate just intervened. Two new kids in a new town, holding on to each other for dear life. I had Danny, too, but sometimes a girl just needs a girlfriend.

We take a few selfies and hashtag the crap out of them before posting them on Instagram. I don't know why we bother; no one ever cares about our shenanigans but us.

We've been laying out for too long—the sun is hot on my skin, and the sparkling water looks too good to resist. I stand and step out of my shorts. My swimsuit is a pale purple, and it's wet in the spots where I've started to sweat. I pull Sam to her feet, and we race to the end of the dock. "On three!" I call out.

Sam counts, "One... two... three!!"

I grab her hand, and we plunge into the water. If this is our last year of school together, we are going to make every second count.

3

Monday Mood

THE FIRST DAY OF school is a blur of schedules, lockers, and nervous excitement. You would think some of these kids hadn't seen each other for years the way they squeal when they see their friends in the hallways. Like they don't update their Instagram every five minutes and stalk each other's pages like crazed fangirls all summer long.

My local Instagram feed is flooded with hashtags like #bestsummerever #bestiesforlife #workingonmytan and #nothinghappensinMcKinleyLake.

I'm not impressed, but they were probably equally unimpressed with the pictures of food and the lake that Sam and I were posting. I think our most-used summer hashtag was #passmeanotherhardshell—no shame in our game.

I've made it through all but my sixth period. My schedule is intense:

Period 1: Math
Period 2: Science

Period 3: History
Period 4: AP English
LUNCH
Period 5: Health
Period 6: Physical Education

My first five classes were all a breeze, but now I have to go to PE. I hate high school physical education classes with a passion. Okay, I slightly enjoyed swimming, but you can only take it once. This year, they've tossed me into something called "Personal Fitness" with Mr. Black, who is also our football team's head coach, and I have no idea what to expect. As a football coach, he's kind of a hard-ass.

I double-check the tape stuck to the combination lock in my hand, quickly memorizing the numbers. I begrudgingly change into the required gym uniform: short, black, skin-tight athletic shorts and our signature red school t-shirt. These shorts remind me of something the volleyball players wear; I don't know how they do it.

I look down at my outfit in mild disgust. Our lovely school colors are crimson and black, but I guess it could be worse. The shirt doesn't even cover the butt of these shorts—which, in my opinion, are too revealing for high school—and no amount of tugging is helping my cause. I sigh, quickly attach the lock, and sprint to the door. As I walk into the gym, I stuff the combination in my bra. The last thing I need is to forget the combination and be stuck in this terrible outfit.

I look up as I pass my fellow crimson-and-black-wearing peers. Everyone is seated on the floor a few feet apart and already in rows. I hurry into a row and take a spot on the cold tile.

Coach Black blows his whistle and demonstrates a sitting leg stretch, instructing us to copy him, followed by more stretching then push-ups. Physical activity like this, that serves no purpose other than sweating, is not my idea of fun. I don't mind playing a sport; it wouldn't be my first choice, but at least it gives me an objective. Soccer, for example—you run after the ball, get the ball, and shoot it at the goal. What is the point of running just to run? You have to force yourself to keep going, either for a set amount of time or until you can't go anymore, and for what? It's not like you win or lose, you just get to say that you ran somewhere. Pointless.

When we've finished warming up to Coach Black's satisfaction, he blows his whistle again. Not that he needs to; we are all standing in front of him, quietly awaiting his next instructions. He clearly wants us to know he's running this show.

"Alright, class." He looks around at us with what can only be described as a sneer. "I imagine you're all out of shape from a summer of couch-potato-ing and binging Netflix, but I intend to whip you all back into shape quickly so we can get to the good stuff. Personal Fitness is my favorite class, and my goal is to have everyone learn what their favorite exercise is by the end of the year. There will be a lot of different physical activities, from weights to team sports, even hiking. Today, we will just be taking a short, two-mile fun run, and to make sure you're not all doing a half-ass job, I'm assigning you a fitness partner this week. I will choose your partners by how well you perform today. If you go slow, I'll make sure you have a partner who will push you. If you're fast and ready to go, I'll be sure to pair you with someone to coach. Make sense?"

A collective groan rings out amongst the students. No one wants a partner they didn't choose, and everyone probably intended to half-ass this run before Coach went and crushed our dreams. He's not like most high school football coaches; he prides himself on being fit and able to do anything he asks of the team. He expects a lot out of them, and that doesn't bode well for me in this class.

"Okay! Follow me, and make it quick!" He chuckles as he jogs out the double doors.

———— ♡ ♡ ♡ ————

I've only just found a good rhythm when I feel someone coming up on me. I'm not exactly at the front of the bunch because I let as many people run out the doors ahead of me as I could. I am not a people person, and I'm not trying to make friends in a class like this.

I hope the person behind me is planning to pass me over and keep going, but I have no such luck. They come up beside me and stay there.

I look up, tearing my eyes from the pavement to see the annoying person who wants to run at my exact pace. I'm startled by the eyes I see peering into mine from above. Brown eyes but so dark they might as well be black. I would know those gorgeous eyes anywhere.

"Hattie, I didn't know you could run without someone yelling 'Fire' first!" He chuckles. Kellan. Danny's best friend, who for all intents and purposes might as well be Older Brother Number Two. Scratch that—I've never had a single brotherly thought about him.

"Ha, funny!" I say, already struggling to keep my breathing steady. I know it has less to do with the physical activity and more to do with his close proximity. He chuckles softly as he keeps pace with me.

I tolerate his teasing constantly; he and Danny really enjoy the sport of it. But I don't trust my thoughts around him, so I try to avoid ever being alone with him for any reason. He makes my palms sweat and my cheeks turn pink.

He's not as muscular or as tall as Danny, but he looks every bit as athletic. His arms are strong, and the veins in his large hands and forearms are prominent. I never knew I could find hands sexy until I saw Kellan's.

His brown hair is a few shades lighter than mine with natural blond highlights, and he's got a slight summer tan on his flawlessly smooth skin. Everything about Kellan is beautiful: his square jaw, chiseled nose, perfectly straight teeth, and that dimple that comes out on his right cheek when he grins.

I've often caught myself sneaking glances at his profile, wondering how it's fair that one person is hogging so much beauty. I've been entirely secretive about my feelings, though—not even Sam knows about this crush. It's mine alone, and that makes it all the more thrilling.

Besides, I can never admit to anyone that I have a crush on Kellan. He's my brother's best friend. What kind of hypocrite would that make me? I banned Sam from even thinking about my brother that way. Best friends are off-limits.

If only my stupid brain would get the memo!

Thing is, he's always been extra nice to me. We have long conversations sometimes about the books I'm reading when he's over at our house. He and Danny invite me to most things: movies, parties, camping trips. The inappropriate feelings I have for him have always been manageable, though, because he never seemed interested in me in that way.

But this summer, things felt different. I swear he looks at me differently now, and sometimes I think he's flirting with me. I can't be sure if it's in my head or some kind of joke to him, though, because he's way out of my league. I bite my lip and try to focus on not tripping over my own feet.

"I didn't realize we had a class together." I bumble over the words—he's making me nervous. And he isn't even doing anything other than running silently beside me with a small smile on his lips.

My eyes linger there—even his lips are beautiful, full and pillowy and probably so very soft. He cocks his head sideways at me, his eyes sparkling as his smile grows, and that damn dimple makes me blush harder.

"Does that bother you or something?" He watches me through thick lashes, and I pray he thinks the burn in my cheeks is from running.

"Not at all. And lucky you—you get the pleasure of my company," I toss back without thinking as I turn my face away. What I want to do is clap a hand over my mouth, but I stifle the urge. What the hell is wrong with me today? Did I just openly flirt with Kellan Anderson? Clearly, the endorphins from exercising are going to my head.

"And you are always a pleasure." He winks at me, and I gawk back at him.

That does it. I stumble over the flat ground and my own clumsy two feet. I let out a little cry, and Kellan reaches out to catch me. But I'm too far gone, so all it does is bring him tumbling down to the ground with me in a twist of motion. I feel the impact of the road biting into my butt and then the added weight of Kellan's body crashing into mine.

I flatten onto the road beneath me. I feel his breath on my neck, his big hands on either side of me, and I'm suddenly hyperaware that his bare skin is touching an impossible amount of my own exposed skin. My chest is pressed tightly against his torso, and if I turn my head at all, I could touch his face with mine.

"Whoa, Hattie, you alright?" His voice laces with concern. My heart hammers, and any hope of sounding normal is dashed away. It's not like we've never touched before—we've known each other for a very long time. We've brushed against each other accidentally before, sat side by side on our couch watching whatever game was on... but right now, my body burns everywhere his body is pressed to mine. Fire, ice, and lightning are striking me simultaneously, and the sensation hurts as much as it feels heavenly.

I hear a moan escape through my lips, and it startles me. I shove against his body hard with both hands. "I'm fine!" I wheeze, my voice betraying me. "Let me up."

He gently lifts himself off me, wiping the dirt from his hands. I climb to my feet, seemingly uninjured... except for my pride, of course—that's been obliterated. He's looking me over, and I am too frazzled to keep standing here. So I do the only thing I can think of: I turn and run.

I sprint ahead with all the gusto I have left in me. I still have about a quarter mile back to the school, but I press on, leaving Kellan behind. He calls after me once, and then I don't hear his voice again. Obviously, I'm losing my mind. There's no way Kellan was flirting with me, and I was definitely out of line with that damn comment.

I make it back quicker than I thought possible, and after logging in my time, I retreat to the locker room like a coward.

———— ◦ ♡ ◦ ————

Sam is waiting for me at my main locker when the final bell rings. Miraculously, I'd slipped out of the gym without running into Kellan. I seriously need this day to end so we can get back to normal—this feels like an alternate universe.

I smile and wave to get Sam's attention as I approach my locker, and she grins back.

"Well, how was an entire day without your bestie?" She laughs. "Complete torture, am I right?"

"I saw you at lunch, Sam."

"That was hours ago. This day has been the longest day in forever, and I am so over it! You feel me?" She slaps my arm playfully.

"You have no idea." I sigh, opening my locker and grabbing my things. "Do we have any plans before we head home today?" I'm hoping she'll say she's tired and take me home. I don't know if I have the energy to avoid spilling my bizarre body-snatchers experience from gym class.

"Want to grab a coffee on the way home and call it?" she asks.

"Now you're speaking my language." I swear she can read my mind sometimes. I'm so thankful.

4

Tricky Tuesday

I READ THE PAGE in front of me for the tenth time, but the words still scramble before my eyes. I'm supposed to be reading all about the health benefits of personal hygiene so I'll be ready for the test tomorrow. I think this is really just a ploy to remind us all not to be stinky, disgusting teenagers. You know, to do the bare minimum: take normal showers and concede that wearing deodorant regularly won't kill us.

There are a few kids in this class who could use the reminder, kids who smell like onions and other things I refuse to name. I completely approve of this assignment. Smart move, Teach.

Danny keeps asking me why I am acting so weird. At dinner last night, Dad grilled us both about our class schedules and his expectations for our grades this year. As if I need any more stress. I just nodded and moved the food around with my fork until he finally excused us from the table.

I'd spent the rest of the night staring at the ceiling. I tried to forget the whole day had ever happened, but each time I closed my eyes, I could feel Kellan's hands on my waist again. I could hear his voice calling my name. If only Danny knew this was the reason for my weirdness.

I've managed to avoid running into Kellan all day, but I know for the next period avoiding him will be impossible. The way his body pressed against mine electrified me, and I can't shake the desire to feel it again. I wonder what would happen if he kissed me.

I can't stop telling myself what a hypocrite I am... stupid teenage hormones.

I even wore my baggiest jeans and school hoodie today, my attempt to blend in with the crowd and appear unaffected and unseen. Kellan would have a hard time believing I wore this outfit for his benefit, if he even saw it. I'll still be forced to put on those ridiculous volleyball shorts for PE... stupid PE.

It's not like this is my first crush; I've even had a boyfriend before. I had a major obsession with Hudson Mayes all through junior high. You wouldn't believe it, but I'd even mustered up the courage to knock on his door and ask him out once. Sam hid just around the corner of his huge brick house, pressed into his mother's rosebushes while I waited for someone to answer.

His little sister opened the door and peered at me while she screamed down the hallway. "Hudson! There's a *girl* here to see you!"

He'd approached the threshold and looked at me with the most translucent blue eyes I'd ever seen. My face burned, and I barely got the words out, but I managed.

"Hi, Hudson. I was wondering if you'd like to go out sometime... you know... with me." My heart lodged in my throat.

"Uh..." He shuffled nervously, running a hand through his wild blond curls. "That's like, really cool of you, but uh... I think I'm just gonna focus on football for now." He'd pulled his little sister away from the door, shoving her toward the hallway he had come from a moment ago, and just stood there, door wide open, with a forced smile on his face.

"Oh, yeah, that's cool. Thanks." My face flushed with heat. I all but ran around the corner to tell Sam.

We'd both squealed and laughed and lived on that high for hours. Sure, he'd turned me down, but I felt like a total badass.

We never did go on any dates after he shut the door in my face. He started dating Tabetha Craine, our school's top mean girl, a few weeks later. I was just thankful that he'd let me down easy. As far as I know, he spared me the humiliation of telling anyone I asked him out, which only made me like him more. Go figure.

Other than my insane crush on Hudson, I've only had one actual boyfriend, Kyle Foster. We met freshman year, and he was the ideal guy in just about every way. He's shy, uncomplicated, and ridiculously smart—we're still friends, for the most part. He's also a dedicated athlete who's shared the same advanced learning classes with me since I moved here.

Sam knew I thought he was cute, so she suggested I ask him to the freshman dance. I laughed her off, but I didn't hate the idea.

In English class, Kyle's desk was conveniently between me and Sam. One afternoon, she leaned over and placed one hand on his desk to get his attention.

"Hey, Kyle, are you going to the dance with anyone?" she said quietly, but not quietly enough, because a few heads turned in our direction.

He shrugged. "No, I haven't asked anyone yet."

"Hattie!" she whisper-screamed, causing more heads to turn. "Are you going to the dance with anyone?"

She knew I wasn't, but I'd figured out her game. Rolling my eyes at her, I played along. "No, Sam."

"Kyle! You should totally go with Hattie!" Sam squealed as if she'd just come up with the most original idea on earth.

Kyle looked at me with excitement in his eyes. "Hattie, do you want to go to the dance with me?"

I did a happy dance in my head—I couldn't help it. Even if Sam had orchestrated the whole thing, he was asking me, and I was thrilled. I'd never imagined it playing out this way. "Yeah, Kyle, I'd like that."

"Okay." He smiled and then went back to his reading.

Sam grinned at me, wiggling her eyebrows, and just like that, I had my first boyfriend.

We dated for a few months, went to the dance, held hands, hugged, talked on the phone. But that was as far as it ever went. We quickly realized we liked each other a lot, but only as friends who had little in common, so we broke it off. We did, however, end on good terms, and I was glad to have had those moments with him.

Danny hated it. But Danny hates most things as they relate to guys—he doesn't think any guy has good intentions. I figure that means he knows from experience what boys are thinking. I'm pretty sure he was wrong about Kyle; I think he's actually just a sweet guy. Danny was overjoyed when Kyle and I called it quits, though; I lied and told him I'd sworn off guys for life to get him off my back. To which he had replied, "I think that's the best idea you've ever had."

But if he knew the things I'd been thinking about Kellan, he'd probably kill us both just to be safe.

This thing with Kellan feels different from anything I've experienced before. It feels intense, and I don't think I'd take rejection from him well. "There won't be any rejection, though, Hattie," I scold myself aloud. "You're not going down that road."

"You say something?" My health partner, Jack, pokes me in the arm with his pencil. He is quiet, and a little strange, but he's smart, so he makes a good partner most of the time.

I look up at him, embarrassed that my thoughts have escaped. I really am losing my mind. "Nah, just reading out loud," I say, hoping he didn't actually hear anything.

He shakes his unruly sandy-brown hair away from his eyes and then goes back to his paper. I sigh in relief just in time for the bell to ring, making me tense again. It's time to go to PE and face the object of my anxiety.

———— ◦ ♡ ◦ ————

I don't linger in the locker room this time, I just slip my gym clothes on and force my feet to move. When I emerge, my classmates are standing in small groups chatting aimlessly with each other, either waiting for Coach or the bell to tell them it's time for class. It smells like feet and sweat in here, just like all gyms—yet another reason I do not want to be in PE.

My stomach is tied up in knots as I scan the gym, looking for Kellan. My feelings are at complete war with each other. I've spent all day hoping to avoid seeing him, but now that I am here and he's not, I feel nothing but disappointment. I find my spot on the floor and sit down. I study the tiles like they might hold all the answers I'm searching for.

The bell rings on cue, and everyone rushes to their spots. Kellan is still mysteriously unaccounted for. Coach takes attendance and pushes us through our stretching and warm-ups until my arms feel shaky and weak from a never-ending barrage of pushups. I really should have spent more time exercising with Danny this summer and less time reading; I am clearly out of shape.

"I have our first football game to prepare for, so I'll be releasing your partner assignments in the next class," Coach announces. "This will be a free period. Half the gym will be for basketball, the other half for soccer. As long as I see you moving, it counts." He waves his hands in the direction of the athletic equipment and retreats into his open office. The gym divider whirrs into action and drops down, separating the gym in two. I help a few of the other students set up soccer goals, and we pick our teams.

By the end of class, I am sweating and laughing, which is a miracle on its own. Sweating doesn't usually make me happy, but we won a very competitive game of soccer, and I scored the last two goals.

Coach lets us out with enough time to rinse off in the showers. I dry my hair with the hand dryer in the girls' locker room. Kristin, a freshman from today's soccer team, watches me curiously as I shake my head back and forth under the hot air.

"Hey," she finally says, motioning toward my head under the nozzle, "that's a neat trick! I never would have thought of that."

"I picked it up from some upperclassman when I took swimming freshman year. I had gym my first period and refused to have wet hair the whole day. Texas frizz is a real style killer—this was my saving grace." I take my mostly dry hair and twist it into a loose side-braid. I smile at her, and she relaxes a little. I remember being a nervous freshman just like her.

"I'll have to give it a try sometime. I hate leaving school all sweaty and gross—it takes over an hour to get home on the bus." She shrugs.

"I don't miss the long bus ride!"

She nods emphatically. "I can't wait to be old enough to drive."

"I get rides from my brother or my friend, Sam, because I don't really drive yet, either. I have my license, but my dad usually gives the car to my brother." I don't know why I'm telling her all this. I'm not usually this talkative with new people.

"Oh, yeah. Danny Tate is your brother, right?" She says it like a question, but it's obvious from the blush in her cheeks she already knows who my brother is. I hide my smile. Another one of his doting fans.

She seems sweet, standing awkwardly and looking sweaty, her copper-brown hair frizzy and loose around her blushing face. She is easily five foot nine, and I start feeling even more hobbit-like than usual. It is one thing to be smaller than all the boys around me, but it's another to be towered over by my girlfriends, too. Kristin wouldn't seem tall next to my brother, though.

"He's my twin brother, actually. You know Danny?" I ask her.

"Um, not really. I've seen him around, though, and someone always seems to be gushing about him or one of his other friends from the team." She pulls out her phone and sits on the bench across from me. "You on Instagram?"

"Yeah, sure. I'm hattietatereads, all one word, if you want to see all my photos of books and food." I laugh.

"Cool, yeah, I'll send you a follow. Maybe we can hang out sometime when we aren't being forced to sweat for a grade."

I nod. I like this girl.

After applying a layer of mascara and some lip gloss, I stare at my own reflection in the wall mirror. I've been social without being awkward—score one for Hattie. But

I can't help wondering where the heck Kellan is. My brain just keeps going back to him.

The bell finally rings, so I say goodbye to Kristin and head for my locker. Sam is already there, as usual. I don't know how she beats me every time, especially since her last class is all the way on the other side of the school, but she does.

"Slumming it with freshmen?" she asks, scrunching up her nose and nodding toward the spot where Kristin had just passed by. "I didn't know we were that desperate for new friends."

I grab my bag from my locker and slam the door, making her jump. "Kristin? She's nice, Sam. I think she was only talking to me because she has a thing for Danny, though." I slide my arm into hers as we walk toward the parking lot.

"Oh, one of his groupies?" She giggles. "They should start a fan club if they haven't already."

I laugh with her.

"Anyway, what's the plan today, gorgeous?" Sam asks. She's wearing a pair of black leggings that meld to her curves like a second skin and an emerald-green polo that accentuates her large chest. Her red hair and green eyes pop when she wears this shade of green, and I'm pretty sure my best friend is the prettiest girl at our school.

"Have I told you how beautiful you are lately?" I ask her.

She pinches my arm. "I look even better with you on my arm, girl. Now let's go get some coffee and blast our eardrums out to some JoBros!"

"That sounds amazing." I grin.

5

After School Activities

DANNY COMES HOME FROM practice around six, and I'm almost finished cooking spaghetti for dinner. After school, I spent an hour listening to Sam tell me all about the cute boys in her classes, and the whole time I couldn't stop thinking about Kellan.

"Yo, Hatts," Danny says as he walks into the kitchen and snatches a piece of garlic bread off the counter. He stuffs it in his mouth whole.

Our kitchen is small for how big our house is, and it feels even smaller with Danny in it. It's technically part of our living room, separated from it by the kitchen island and three bar stools, the only seating available. The sink is on the wall opposite the island, a dishwasher beside it, and the stove and fridge are on the side wall next to a small pantry. That's about it. All business, no frills. Dad didn't bother decorating when we moved in, so it's crisp white and sterile-looking, and we don't even own a real kitchen table. But it's only the three of us, so I guess it works out okay.

"Dinner is just about ready," I say, a cloud of hot steam billowing around me as I pour the noodles into a strainer over the sink. Dad left a note saying he might be home extra late tonight, and he hoped I wouldn't mind taking care of the cooking.

Danny never gets home before six on school nights. Luckily, my homework load hasn't started feeling rough just yet, and pasta doesn't take much time or effort to throw together. When dinner is left to me, we eat a lot of pasta.

Danny comes back just as I finish plating the food wearing boxer shorts with footballs on them and a white t-shirt, his idea of pajamas. This is a good sign—it means he will want to hang out and have a chill night after dinner. I want that, too. My arms are still aching from the pushups earlier, and my mind is still on Kellan. I've been trying to think of a way to ask about him without tipping big brother off all afternoon.

"How was practice?" I ask instead.

Danny's dark hair is wet from the shower, and he flings water at me as he shakes his head. "You know, Coach is a hard-ass. Someone forgot to put their phone on silent, and when he heard it ringing, he made us run two extra miles as punishment. So now I'm starving, and I have jello legs. Who calls anyone anymore, anyway? Haven't they heard of texting?"

I try not to roll my eyes. God forbid someone uses a phone for its intended purpose.

"Sit, then. I just need to get us something to drink." I busy myself with grabbing glasses from the cupboard and filling them with ice and water. I slide them across the island and then join him on the other side. Even though Dad isn't here, I take my normal stool next to Danny's and inhale the rich smells of garlic and tomato coming off my plate.

We eat in silence for a while, and Danny all but licks his plate as he empties it. Football wears him out and makes him ridiculously hungry. He reminds me of a wild animal most nights, inhaling his food unapologetically and loud like a high-powered vacuum. I have barely finished half of my pasta when he asks for seconds. I'm just glad someone thinks my cooking is worth a second helping.

After dinner, he helps me wash the dishes and put them away. Dad still isn't home, but that's the norm around here. "Wanna watch a few episodes of *Teen Wolf*?" I ask. We started the first season on Netflix a few months ago, and we're totally hooked on binging the old MTV show.

"Yeah. Want me to set it up in my room?" Danny asks.

I look at him closely. He looks exhausted—he only suggests we chill in his room if he's extra tired. He likes to puff up all the pillows on his bed and flop on top of them while we watch. We get extra comfortable and usually fall asleep by the second episode. Dad has been known to carry me to my own room when he gets home. Trying to wake me up is pointless—once I'm out, I'm out.

Nights like these are some of my favorites. Danny lets me hang out in his room like we did when we were younger and completely inseparable. The love I have for my brother is the strongest out of all my relationships; he's the one person that I never doubt will always be there for me.

"Sure. Let me just change into my PJs and call Sam real quick," I answer, rushing down the hall before he can protest.

"Tell Sam she'll live without a goodnight call every dang night!" I hear him call after me, but I ignore him.

I don't talk to Sam for long. I tell her Danny is wiped out, and I want to get at least one episode in before he falls asleep. We agree to just talk in the morning.

I slip into my favorite pair of pajamas: a pair of lavender cotton shorts and a matching tank top. Uncle Dan sent them to me for Christmas last year. Then I run through our shared bathroom and into his room.

Danny's room is mostly devoid of decoration. He sides with Dad on the whole minimalist mindset. His walls are painted a light gray, the color of an overcast sky. He has a white bookshelf that holds a few books, his video game collection, and all his sports trophies neatly lined up on the top shelves. He also has a secret stack of journals that he keeps hidden in his closet. Journals that he doesn't think anyone knows about.

His queen-sized bed is covered in a midnight-blue comforter and four matching, larger-than-life pillows. The nightstand on the left side holds only a lamp. His TV sits directly across from his bed, and the desk under his one window is clean and tidy. Even his laptop is closed and centered perfectly in the middle of his desk. I wish I was as naturally organized as my brother. That will never happen.

Danny has *Teen Wolf* ready to go, and he's sitting cross-legged on one side of the bed with a bowl of popcorn in his lap. "Wow, I'm surprised Sam let you off the phone so fast. I made myself a snack, because I figured you two had a whole life story to tell each other before bed tonight."

I climb onto the other side of his bed and snuggle under the comforter. "I told her you don't think we need nightly phone calls, and she says you're an ass."

"Just like her to be thinking about my ass. I know she loves me—no way she said that." His eyes narrow at me, and he hits me on the head with one of his pillows.

"You wish. She likes a lot of guys. Unfortunately, your name never comes up." I don't add it's because I've forbidden it.

"Ha! You can't lie to me—I can see it on your face. She *does* like my hot ass." He leans over to tickle me, and I squeal, trying to get away but trapped in the comforter.

"Yeah, she probably thinks about your ass as much as Kellan thinks about mine." I immediately cover my mouth with my hand. What the hell? This is what happens when I can't get something out of my head; eventually, it sneaks out of my traitorous mouth. I sit up and pull my hair tie out, busying myself with redoing my braid.

"Kellan better not be thinking anything about your ass!" Danny glares at me. "Did he say something to you?"

"NO!" I yell, quickly attempting to rein him in. "It was just a joke—like he would, anyway." Kellan probably has as much interest in me as I have in running. Yesterday was all in my head, and I need to move the heck on. Now I'm starting crap even though there's nothing to tell, and Danny looks mad as hell. "I didn't even see him today—was he at practice?"

Curse my brain. *This is not the time to pump your brother for information!* I lay back down on the bed.

Danny relaxes a little but keeps his gaze locked on me, his eyes darkening with suspicion. "Yeah, he was. Coach had him running errands during sixth period. I know you have a class with him this year—why didn't you tell me?"

I try to think of a good excuse for not telling him, but, to be honest, I'm not sure why I didn't just mention it on Monday after school when Dad was grilling us about our classes. Probably because I was still unsure about our weird contact during the run and my conflicting feelings afterward. If it was no big deal, why hadn't I been able to stop thinking about it for a single minute since he fell on top of me?

"Forgot, I guess. It's PE—you know I hate that class. I try to forget everything that happens there. Besides, there's this freshman in my class who clearly has the hots for you and probably *does* think you have a hot ass," I say, trying to distract him.

"Freshman? Who?" He takes the bait, and I sit up triumphantly.

"Kristin something, cute girl, tall, curly hair, freckles? Maybe you have a class together or something?" I watch his cheeks turn pink.

"Nah, don't think so. It doesn't matter, anyway; I'm not interested in dating right now. I just want to focus on the team and then leave for college without relationship drama, ya know? It is kind of flattering, though." He winks at me, and I slug him in the arm. He doesn't need any flattery—his ego is plenty big enough of its own accord. "Are you trying to date someone this year?" he asks.

I chew on my bottom lip. Am I? Am I hoping that I can find a boyfriend this year? Maybe experience my first kiss?

Absolutely.

I'm not sure I can say this to Danny, though, because when I close my eyes and think about the scenario, I can only see one pair of gorgeously plump lips touching mine, and they belong to Kellan Anderson.

"I don't know—why do you care?" I ask instead.

"I care because I'm your brother, Hatts, and I don't want some stupid loser idiot breaking your heart. I don't even want to think about some guy groping my sister—it freaks me out." He flexes. "Just wait until we get to college or something. Hopefully, guys are more mature by then, and at least then I won't have to see it."

Unless I follow him to college like I intend to.

"So let's be clear: It's not really my heart you're worried about—you just don't want to think about your sister kissing someone?" I smooth my hands over his comforter, thinking about what he said.

"No, you don't need to date anyone." He adds quietly, "I better not catch anyone even thinking about touching you. Just focus on school and forget about guys. You'll thank me later." For some reason, that last comment has me reeling.

"Danny, are you a virgin?" I ask. I already know he's not, but I have a point to make. His face instantly goes pink; it's a family trait.

"Where are you going with this, Hatts? No, I'm not a virgin... but what the hell kind of question is that?" He looks uncomfortable.

"Then don't you dare start acting like you have any say in what I do with my body. We might have shared the womb, but this is my body. It's my decision what I do or don't do with it." I stare back at him. No way is he going to make me feel like he has the last word in my dating life. I feel a fire spark in my veins.

"You're thinking about sleeping with someone?" He grips the popcorn bowl in his hands so hard his knuckles turn white, his lips pulling into a tight line as his jaw clenches.

He's glaring at me, and I glare right back. This isn't the stone age; girls shouldn't be held to some archaic standard of virginity and purity just to appease the men in their lives. I haven't been thinking about sleeping with anyone—I haven't even had my first kiss yet—but how is any of that his business? News flash—it's not! "I mean, I haven't, but if I want to, then I will, and you better not have anything to say about it unless I ask for your opinion!" I shout while I climb out of his bed. I cannot sit here another second. I'm angry, and my fists are clenched as I stalk back toward my room. Just before I leave, I yell over my shoulder, "Guys are such hypocrites!" and rattle the walls as I slam the door behind me.

6

Fighting Fury

HOT TEARS SPILL DOWN my cheeks, soaking my bed. I punch the pillow as if the damp heap of cotton is to blame. I just wanted to spend some time with my brother, maybe get some advice on my strange feelings for Kellan. I wanted to dig for some information about the guy I've known for many years but who suddenly feels like an enigma.

Our fight broke out so fast, and nothing makes me feel sicker than unresolved arguments, especially with Danny—he's my other half. I'm naturally a peacekeeper. The fact that I'm always apologizing first drives Sam crazy—she says I have to stop being everyone's doormat.

Usually, I'll do whatever it takes to make things feel normal again, but something is stopping me now. No matter how much I hate that Danny and I are fighting, he's the one who's wrong this time, and I refuse to back down.

I respect Danny. His approval is something that I seek constantly; I truly value his opinion. I can't remember a time when I haven't looked to him for guidance. When something is hard or scary, Danny is my security blanket, the voice of reason in my head even when he's not physically around. Sometimes I hate his big, dumb face, but I always love him unconditionally. Right now, however, I'm wishing my mother was here for some girl talk... and the thought surprises me.

I punch my pillow again and flip the damp side over. I wipe furiously at the tears on my face. I will not keep crying about this—I don't cry for stupid things. I'm not that kind of girl. So instead, I slide out of bed and look around my messy room.

My walls are a pale yellow, the color of lemon sorbet, my favorite dessert. There are books everywhere, stacked in piles, peeking out from under my twin bed, toppling over on my nightstand. My bookshelf in the corner is mostly bare and neglected. I've been lazy about returning my books to their homes, content with devouring them and leaving them where they fell.

They deserve better.

There's no way I'm going to sleep, so I might as well clean this mess up. Dad would have a lot to say about the mess if he was ever home long enough to notice it—and I could use the distraction, anyway.

I try to get out of my head, to turn off my mind and just work, but my thoughts still drift to my mother.

Mom took off sometime before our sixth birthday. I remember Dad sitting down with Danny and me, looking strange and red-faced.

"Motherhood was suffocating her. Her words, not mine," he'd said. That was the most we could expect out of him on the subject. He's just not a talker when it comes to emotional things.

I don't remember her much anymore. Danny cried for her for weeks, begging her to come back. Calling Dad names and asking him why he wouldn't find Mom and bring her home. He thought Dad must have locked her out of the house or forgot to pick her up from work.

Six-year-olds don't have the capacity to understand that a mother can abandon her own children. They don't understand that sometimes people hurt you and don't come back to apologize for it. I think it happens a lot more often than we think it does, but people just don't like to talk about it.

I just stopped talking completely. For the entire summer, I didn't utter a single word; Danny did all the talking for the both of us. I hid behind him in every way possible. It frustrated Nana that I wouldn't open up to anyone.

Nana was never one to mince her words. She told me what she thought about Mom leaving over dinner one night. "She didn't ever love you," Nana said between bites of her famous lasagna. "She was broken, and her heart didn't work right. She only knew how to love herself."

Once Danny stopped crying for Mom, it was like she never existed. Nana took down all her pictures, and school started back up. First grade began, and we got to ride the bus to school.

Giving us more independence was the perfect distraction. I loved school, and it was the only thing that got me talking again.

Nana moved in and stayed with us for a few years. Dad still had to go on deployments; the Army doesn't wait because your wife leaves you. They just told Dad to figure out his childcare situation and get on with it. So he went to Afghanistan, Iraq, and so many countries he couldn't even tell us about. Someone had to look after us, so Nana did the best she could.

I don't remember crying for my mother. I'm sure that's weird, and maybe I just blocked it out, but what I do remember is climbing into Danny's bed and holding onto him like he might disappear into the night like she had. He never did, but I think I slept in his room every night for two years before I was convinced. Danny never kicked me out, either—I think he needed that reassurance just as much as I did.

Dad loves us, whatever his version of love is. He takes care of us. All of our physical needs are met. He isn't a hugger or a talker. Mostly he lays down rules and laws and leads by example. We have always been fed and dressed in nice clothes. We've lived in nice houses and played sports or whatever else we wanted to participate in.

Nana doted on us as much as she could. She always thought Dad was broken, too. She seemed to think that Mom leaving, and the things he'd seen in war, had made him harder. That all his trapped feelings had broken his wings and made him a caged animal. She'd frown sometimes out of nowhere and say, "You poor dears. Not enough love in this house." It wasn't a question, just a statement under her breath. I still don't know what she meant by that.

An hour later, my books are meticulously organized on my shelves by the author's last name, and my nerves have calmed. Not a single book is out of place in my room, and I've picked up all my dirty clothes as well as started a load of laundry. My room is clean, and my fluffy purple comforter is calling my name, but as I pad over to my bed, I hear a soft knock on the bathroom door.

"Hatts? You still up?" I hear Danny's deep voice through the door. What does he want now? I've cried enough for one night. I whip the door open and stare at him standing on the other side. He takes a breath and rubs a hand over his jaw, looking as tired as I feel.

"I'm up, but I'm about to go to sleep, so what the heck do you need?" I put a hand on my hip and stand as tall as I can, which is not nearly tall enough to meet my brother's height, but it does make me feel more equal.

"I'm sorry, Hatts, I was out of line," he says quietly. "You're right—if you want to date someone, it's not really my business. I just worry about you. You're the most amazing girl I know, and there are a lot of creeps out there." One side of his mouth quirks up, and his thick hair is sticking out in every direction as his eyes watch my every move. He holds on to both sides of the doorjamb and does a few standing push-ups, waiting for my response. He is annoying and rude, but I also see the adorable brother that I love.

"Did hell freeze over?" I gape at him with exaggerated shock. "Because I believe you just apologized to your twin without someone forcing you to for the first time ever."

"Can you be serious for a second?" He growls a little before reining it back in and stepping inside my room. He puts both of his big hands on my shoulders and leans down to meet my eyes. "I love you. I'm sorry. It just makes me crazy thinking about someone hurting you. I've always had your back—I still do. I just want you to know I'm here when you need me."

I want to hold on to my anger, but I feel it seeping from my bones. He's not good at talking about his emotions—no one in this family is—and he's never been the first to apologize. I decide to accept this win. I take a step closer and wrap my arms around his neck in a hug.

"I love you, too, jerkface. Just don't be so pushy about my personal life." I sigh. I recognize this could be the perfect moment to come clean about Kellan, but I take the coward's way out and stay silent.

7

Let's Get Quizzical

I GROAN OUT LOUD on Wednesday morning when my alarm blares at 0500. After Danny came to my room to make up, we'd both gone to bed. I laid under the covers for another hour, lost in my thoughts, before falling asleep and suffering through strange dreams. I'm not a morning person, and I don't do well on very little sleep. So I'm tempted to hit snooze and skip my shower, but Dad chooses that moment to stick his head in my doorway.

"Good morning, Hattie. I made some chai tea if you'd like some before school."

My eyes try to focus on his face, but they're still bleary, and he looks fuzzy. He's already dressed for work, that much I can tell—dark dress pants and a royal-blue polo with his company logo on it. I don't know when he finds time to sleep. He must have come home pretty late, because I never heard him come in last night.

"Sure, Dad, I'll be out in a minute," I say with more enthusiasm than I feel. I'm extra glad I cleaned my room last night. Dad wouldn't be so cheery this morning had I not.

I pray that the hot shower will lighten my sour mood.

When I finally sit on my stool in the kitchen, both Dad and Danny are already eating breakfast. Oatmeal for Dad—so gross—and two slices of toast with peanut butter plus a bowl of fruit for Danny. My spot has a nice, hot cup of vanilla chai tea waiting for me. Dad reaches over and pours just the right amount of french vanilla creamer into my cup; I stir it in, watching the liquid change from a muddy brown to a milky-cream color.

I feel a little more human after my shower. I took the time to dry and curl my hair. I even added a little mascara and lip gloss, and after a little concealer, you can only *slightly* see the black rings under my eyes. I decided on a pair of white jeans and a black v-neck t-shirt today, so the only pop of color in my outfit will be my signature crimson Chucks.

"So, Dad," Danny says, "You're coming to our first game this Friday?" He takes a huge bite of toast, and I try not to grimace at his chomping.

I hate the sound of people eating, chewing, and lip-smacking. I learned at school that I'm not alone in that feeling—it's actually a disorder called misophonia. I like knowing there are other people out there who understand the goosebumps that break out over my body when I hear people chew.

Geez. I feel like a real bear today.

"I'll be at the game," Dad says between bites of oatmeal. "I have a few things going on Friday with a new group of recruits, and I have a meeting at Fort Hood with the transition department, but I should be done around lunch. I'll have more than enough time to make it. We can go out for pizza afterward. Both of you can bring some friends."

When Dad says he will have enough time, it usually means he's going to be late. With the military, time seems to have a different meaning.

I take my first sip of tea and close my eyes as the warm liquid moves through my body. A little caffeine jolt before school is exactly what I need, and nothing else could taste as good as this for my fix.

"When does Uncle Dan get back from Afghanistan?" I ask. Dan isn't really our uncle in the traditional sense; he's part of our military family. He and Dad have been battle buddies since they met in Basic Training years ago, long before we were born. He's our only godparent, and he's Danny's namesake. Now he works as Dad's right-hand man. He definitely feels like family, and he's actually fun to be around. He doesn't take things as seriously as Dad does, and it's delightful to see Dad loosen up a little when he's here.

Dad is at the sink, washing his bowl and tidying up the kitchen. Everything is always extra clean and tidy when Dad is around. He answers me as he dries the dishes. "Rotation ends next month, so he should be back by

Thanksgiving. I thought I'd invite him over again this year. He's seeing that woman now; I suppose we should invite her, too."

"That woman has a name, Dad." I laugh because I almost feel like he's jealous of her hanging around. "Melissa seems like a genuinely nice lady, and it's been over a year now. I think she's a permanent fixture."

Dad's eyes crinkle at the corners, and his forehead creases in thought; he leans back against the sink and folds his arms over his chest. "I suppose it has been awhile now."

Danny crosses the kitchen and tosses his plate in the sink before matching Dad's stance. They look comical this way, the two of them side by side. I wouldn't say they look identical, but Danny is definitely the younger version of Dad. Dad's silver locks aren't as long as Danny's spiked hair, but his hair is long for him and sticking up in the same spots. Dad keeps himself in good shape, but Danny's muscles bulge in his shirt sleeves a little more prominently. They are the same height and are both tanned from long hours spent outdoors.

Where Danny's skin is full and unblemished, Dad wears the scars of a hard life. There are wrinkles and hard lines etched into his skin. But they're both handsome to me—each has strikingly strong features that wouldn't look out of place on a movie screen or a magazine cover.

"What do you think, Dad?" Danny asks. He wiggles his eyebrows comically at me. "Is it time for you to find your own lady friend?"

Dad chuckles. "What I think..." He steps away from the counter as he continues, "... is that it's time for the two of you to head to school." We laugh together and go our separate ways.

Sam and I are sitting at a table in the cafeteria at lunch. I'm enjoying a nice soft pretzel, and Sam has splurged for the Walking Taco, which smells really enticing. It's basically a bag of corn chips they pour chili and cheese into before sending you off with a spoon. It's hard to eat daintily, but she pulls it off pretty well. When I eat things like that, I end up wearing them. Wearing a Walking Taco is one thing, but wearing it in white jeans is a whole different story. I decided not to risk it.

"It doesn't feel like the first week of school." Sam turns to me. "Last year, we had so many fun things going on! This year blows."

I finish chewing my pretzel and take a drink of water. I look around the cafeteria and see that most of the tables are occupied now, but everyone's chatting quietly. The atmosphere does seem to be lacking an exciting buzz this year. "I think lunch feels boring now since they broke us up by grades."

She nods at my hypothesis, taking more perfectly dainty bites of her lunch.

Our high school is the only one in the area, so it's filling up quickly as the little town grows in population. Since there are so many of us, they stagger our lunch periods by grade. They also closed our campus, so we can't leave to go to lunch anymore. Not having the entire school in one place at lunch makes for a lot less chaos, but lunch also feels a little boring now.

"I don't just mean lunch, though—the whole start of school feels lame so far. Where's the excitement?" she huffs.

"There's the first season game this Friday." I shrug, reminding her. The preseason games are over, but we don't usually get too excited about those, anyway. The games are more fun to watch once the guys get their competitive spirits roaring.

"Ooh, yeah! What are we doing that night?" Her hands brush over her hair, and she turns sideways on the bench to face me. "Let's do our hair and makeup together and see what hotties we can talk to at the game!"

"I didn't plan on anything less, bestie." I laugh. "Dad said he'll take us out for pizza afterward."

"That man is always feeding me, which almost makes up for his iron fist." She smirks.

"Have you seen Danny?" What I really want to ask is if she's seen Kellan, but I'm not ready to give all that away just yet. I don't know why, but I still want to keep it to myself. I feel a little guilty about that but not enough to spill my guts.

"No, I don't see any of the team actually." She scans the room. "Coach probably has them sacrificing a goat to the football gods or something."

I laugh, which makes me choke on the water I was drinking. She slaps my back as I cough.

"What? He's nuts about games, so I wouldn't put it past him. You know it's true." She shrugs.

I wonder if Kellan is going to be missing in action at PE again, and I spend the rest of lunch wondering what I'll even say the next time I see him.

———— ♡ ♡ ♡ ————

"Oh, hey!" is what comes out of my mouth. I stumble out of the girls' locker room with my new friend, Kristin, right behind me and run right into Kellan's backside. I place a hand awkwardly against his shoulder to steady myself after my abrupt stop. The heat coming off of him nearly burns me.

He turns around quickly and holds me still. "Keep falling into my arms, and I might develop a hero complex," he crows. His gorgeous, black-brown eyes wash over my body and then come back to mine. I feel myself blush as if he has physically touched the path his eyes followed with his hands. He's wearing our lame gym attire, but on him it looks natural. I feel like stealing a pair of my brother's gym shorts and wearing them in protest. Why do the girls' shorts have to be so indecent while the boys basically get typical basketball shorts?

I steady myself and take a small step back. "Ha, so funny." My voice shakes. I've talked to this boy a million times in my life, so why is he suddenly throwing me off-kilter?

"Coach is about to post the gym partners list if he can figure out how to print it. I swear he lives to torture everyone." Kellan motions to where the coach in question is perched at his desk. He has some dorky-looking glasses on, and he's glowering at his computer with absolute concentration.

I forgot we were getting assigned partners—I've been too busy worrying about this interaction. Now I'm even more convinced that I've imagined the whole weird vibe, that Kellan still sees me as Danny's annoying twin sister and nothing more. He doesn't seem nervous or caught off guard at all; in fact, I'm the only one acting like a complete dork right now.

I turn to Kristin. "I'd say I wish you were my partner, but Coach already warned us it's boy-girl partners only. I'm kind of surprised he didn't make us stay with our own genders—he strikes me as the sexist type." I motion to my gym uniform. "Pretty sure these needed his approval."

Kristin giggles and looks between me and Kellan a few times. "I don't mind the uniform so much. It could be worse, I'm sure. My cousin has to wear an orange sweat suit at her school, and it's an all-girls school. So extra. Someone even posted pictures of them on Instagram." She trembles. "Remind me, and I'll show you sometime. It's bad."

Coach comes out of his office and blows his whistle. He has a sheet of paper in his hand, and he's looking rather proud of himself.

"Crap, guess he figured out the printer." Kellan winks, and we all head to our assigned tiles.

"Okay, class, partners have been chosen. I will not make any changes for any reason, so deal with it. I'm going to tape it to the wall here. Boys, you come up and find your partner's name and then head out for a nice, brisk walk and get to know each other a little bit. There may be a quiz at the end of the week, so no slacking. Principal Mack says I don't make you kids do enough social exercises to get to know each other or some new age hippy baloney, so this should kill two birds with one stone." He huffs like he's being put out and waves his hands in the air before taping the paper to the wall. He blows his whistle again—as if we haven't all seen him do it—and stomps back to his office.

I lean back on my hands and wait as the boys bum-rush the posting like it's the starting lineup. Kristin is paired with Josh Campbell, one of our best track runners but who is also five four at best. She towers over him, and I catch her eye as she heads out the door, looking miserable. She's probably not into running just like me and knows she's in for a real workout this year.

"Let's go," Kellan says, offering his hand to me.

"I'm waiting for my gym partner," I say, not bothering to reach back.

"I am your partner, Hattie." He thrusts his hand forward again.

My eyebrows pull together, and I grip his offered hand. "What did you do, rig the list?"

"Maybe I did... I do a lot of things for Coach when he's busy planning for games." He winks at me again as he pulls me to my feet. His hand sends shocks through my arm. His touch is like a drug, and when he finally drops my hand, I'm already craving my next hit.

"Why would you want to be stuck with me? I run slower than my nana." I laugh, walking toward the doors with him.

His eyes are sparkling with mischief as he shakes his head. "You don't like to run, but you're not slow. Plus, I thought it might be fun." He shrugs, and I think his first comment must be referring to me running away from him on Monday. I'm not sure what he means by the fun part.

We step outside, and I'm hit with a burst of sticky air. Summer hasn't officially surrendered to fall in Texas, and the humidity is unforgiving. The wind blows, and the leaves in the trees dance, casting melodic shadows across the pavement.

Our school sits in the most beautiful part of the town surrounded by ancient, looming trees that have just started turning colors. Brilliant oranges, yellows, and reds sway and flutter above our heads. The houses in this area are old and weary. More than one near the school has a porch in desperate need of renovation, but all of the houses seem charming this time of year, like they would be the perfect setting for a Halloween festival or a Hallmark movie. Further down the road, at the top of the hill, parts of the lake peek through the trees. It's an awe-inspiring view, perfect for a walk or run if you're into that sort of thing. Even I'm entranced by the romance of it all for a moment.

"I love this time of year," Kellan says, shaking me from my thoughts. He's walking close to my side, letting me set the pace. Our hands swing dangerously close to each other with each stride. I keep hoping they'll brush so I can have another hit of that electricity that hums between us.

"Me, too," I say, and I can't help but smile. Even if I've caught some strange new buzz of feelings for this boy, he's still the same Kellan that hangs around with my brother. "So did Coach tell you what kind of things we're supposed to know about each other for his quiz?"

Kellan lets out a loud belly laugh. "There isn't a quiz. He only said that so word will get back to Principal Mack, and he'll get off his back. Coach doesn't do paper grading. He says he doesn't believe in paperwork for physical activity."

"What's your favorite color?" I ask anyway, since this is the perfect excuse to ask anything I want. I already know his favorite color is red, but I still wait eagerly for his response.

"Red. Your favorite is purple." He shakes his head with a slight smile on his face. "But if you want to play this game, I'm down. What do you like to do besides read all those books?"

We do know a lot about each other already—he's right about that—but there are things I've never asked him before. "I like to binge-watch TV shows and daydream about writing for one someday. Preferably on the CW network; that's where all my favorites are... except *Teen Wolf*." I live for the teen drama, and if they add in some supernatural stuff, I'm hooked. "My turn! What do you want to do after high school?"

He stops walking and looks out over the hill as we reach the top—the water I can see through the trees is sparkling in the afternoon sun. He turns to me, tense, his eyebrows bunched together. "I want to play football in college and then maybe coach at a school. I don't really have a desire to go pro or anything like that, but being a high school gym teacher sounds like a dream job to me."

"I can actually see that. I think you'd be a great coach." I think he could be great at just about anything. He was always rallying the kids together for something when we were younger, so he is a natural at entertaining a crowd.

He's the youngest of the five Anderson boys, the last one at home now. His older brothers have all gone off to college.

Coming from such a big, loving family has shaped him into a fine young man. Kellan's mom and dad are pretty wonderful, too.

He turns back toward me. "I'd watch a show that you wrote for, even if it turns out to be 'chick TV.'"

"What is 'chick TV'? I think you mean 'good TV.'"

He laughs. "Call it what you will."

"Just ask another question, Kellan."

"Who was the last guy you kissed?" he asks with a lopsided grin.

"Hard pass." I laugh. "You?"

"I haven't kissed any guys, actually." He smirks, and I smack his arm playfully. I haven't either, but I don't say that out loud.

I'm hot and sweaty, and my shorts are riding up my thighs. I tug on them hopelessly. "These uniforms are such a joke."

"They have pants; you just have to request them." Kellan shrugs as if it's common knowledge.

"Pants?" I ask incredulously. "Like all-the-way-past-my-ankles pants?" I grab his arm for emphasis then quickly pull away. I can't stop finding excuses to touch him.

"Yeah, black yoga pants for the girls and athletic-style ones for the guys. They have the form in the main office—just ask the attendance lady for one."

"Oh, yes, that is so happening," I say triumphantly. Yoga pants! I can get on board with that. I definitely would have recalled seeing those on the order form Coach gave us, and they were not an option. I'm annoyed that there's a separate form and I had no idea.

"You'd look good in yoga pants," he says, and I swear I see him blush a little. "Forget I said that; it came out creepy."

"I don't think you're a creep. I'll take the compliment." But the comment makes me question his motives again. So I turn and sprint back down the hill. He doesn't miss a beat and quickly matches my pace.

"I thought you said you run slower than your nana," he says once he catches up to me.

"Well, I'm sweating like a pig out here, and I want to get this over with, so let's see if you can keep up." I'm also feeling confused and uncomfortable, and I'm running from my feelings as usual.

We surprisingly run the last half-mile in silence. Maybe this won't be so bad after all.

———— ♡ ————

After school, I have Sam drop me off at home so I can get some house chores done. I turn on some loud music, pop my headphones in, and go to town. With the game coming up this Friday, I don't want anything left to do before the weekend. I scrub the bathrooms until they shine, knocking out my least favorite job first. I fold and distribute the clean laundry—the amount of clothes we have is staggering, and I'm surprised any of us have clean underwear left in our drawers. Then I vacuum the house from back to front, swaying and singing loudly as I go.

I'm on the last part of the living room when I feel someone tap on my shoulder, and I jump out of my skin. "Holy crap!" I scream as I whip around, yanking my earbuds from my ears and stabbing at the vacuum's switch to turn it off.

Danny is bent over with his hands on his knees, laughing so hard he's almost crying. Directly behind him, Kellan is grinning at me, laughter sparkling in his eyes.

"Sorry to interrupt your show, Hattie," my brother jokes, still catching his breath.

I slug him in the arm. "Ugh, you're such a jerk. I'm cleaning *our* house if you didn't notice. You'd better be nice, or I'll clean a toilet with your toothbrush." I mime the action for emphasis, and he sobers a little.

"Brutal." He surrenders with his hands in the air. "I was just going to ask if you want me to order Chinese tonight."

"I was going to cut up veggies from the fridge before they go bad. How do you feel about egg scrambles? I'll do the egg stuff if you'll make the bacon?" I am terrible at cooking bacon—the ordeal always ends in smoke—and Danny knows it.

My words fly out a little faster than normal. I'm trying not to let him or Kellan see how embarrassed I am. I'm mortified they caught me dancing and belting out Taylor Swift in the living room. My cheeks are probably as red as a tomato.

"Sounds like a deal. We got enough for Kellan to stay? Practice was rough—we are starving." He looks back at Kellan, who nods.

"Hey, Hattie." Kellan flashes me a smile with those perfectly straight teeth. They're both wearing shorts and t-shirts and have damp hair; they must have showered in the locker rooms before coming here. Kellan's cheeks are flushed, and he looks adorable leaning against the back of the couch.

I try not to stare too long, but it takes some real effort to shift my gaze back to Danny. "Yeah, we have plenty of food. I'll finish this vacuuming and start chopping veggies. Let me know when you're ready to start the bacon. Oh, and Dad says he'll be home early tonight."

"Early like before the sun comes up?" Danny deadpans.

"Good one." I don't laugh, but it is funny.

"Give me like ten minutes, and I'll get it started. I just want to sit down for a little while." He looks beat.

I nod at him and put my headphones back in, turning around to finish up the vacuuming. I am extra careful not to shake my booty this time, especially with Kellan here and Danny watching.

Getting through dinner without making googly eyes at Kellan may prove harder than expected. I don't know when everything changed, but given the smile Kellan flashed at me just a few minutes ago, I am certain that it has.

Now I just have to keep it under wraps.

———— ♡ ♡ ♡ ————

I finish chopping the green onion, tomato, and bell pepper fairly quickly. Then I shred the cheese with our ancient torture device of a cheese grater.

Danny still hasn't come out of his room to fry the bacon. I rinse my hands in the sink and head down the hall, stopping just before I get to his door when I hear him and Kellan talking. Eavesdropping is rude, but it's also a little sister's duty, isn't it?

"So did you see Sarah in Lit today? Damn, she got hot over the summer," Danny says. I feel my body tense.

Kellen clears his throat. "She's alright." I bite back a smile. Good, he's not impressed by that utterly gorgeous blonde human. Although I'm not sure why. Even I'm not immune to her beauty. "I've noticed she's not the only one who changed over the summer."

"Oh, yeah? Who else did I miss?" Danny asks. I'm not sure I want to hear the answer to that. Kellan having a crush on someone is totally none of my business, but suddenly I feel possessive and a little jealous.

"Hattie sure has grown up."

I freeze. They must know I'm out here, and they're messing with me. My face instantly heats, and my ears prick.

"What the actual hell, dude! Shut your mouth," Danny yells, followed by what can only be described as awkward scuffling.

"You have to know your sister is hot, dude." I hear laughing and more thumping.

"Your mom is hot, bro."

"Seriously? That's the best you got?" I can almost hear the eye roll through the door, and I cover my mouth to keep from laughing.

"People go missing around here all the time, Kel. You know what my dad does for a living, right? How about I call and tell him what you just said about his precious daughter and see what happens? I'll cry for you when your face shows up on a milk carton."

"You won't do it—you're all talk." Kellan's voice cracks.

"Alright, but you asked for it..." I hear Danny heading for the door, and I hold my breath.

"Alright, alright," Kellan yells out. "I'll stop."

I hear more scuffling and heavy breathing then laughter. "Is something going on with you two or something, Kel? Seriously?"

"Nah, bro." My heart drops a little. I know there's nothing going on, but I think I want there to be. I turn to head back to the kitchen. I'll make the bacon myself; I'm not walking in on that conversation.

Just as I walk away, I hear one last heartbreaking exchange.

"Good. Don't be that guy. You might be my best friend, but she's my sister—she's off-limits."

"Yeah, man, I know the deal."

Yeah, I know the deal, too, but I'm really starting to hate it.

8

Tongue Twister

I'M STILL REPLAYING THE conversation between Kellan and Danny in my head when I enter the gym on Thursday. I can't stop hearing Kellan say there's nothing going on between us. Because I swear there is. I'm not the kind of girl who makes things up like this, right? I guess I *am* the type of girl who stands outside her brother's bedroom door listening in on conversations I have no business hearing. I'm kicking myself for being nosy. Why can't I be like Sam and have no regrets?

I drag my sneakers across the polished gym floor. Having heard Kellan say he wouldn't act on his feelings weighs heavier on my mind than I thought possible. I guess this innocent little crush I have on him is more serious than I thought. Maybe it isn't so innocent. Maybe I really like him. Actually, I know I do. What I don't know is how to keep Danny from getting in the way.

I pull on my shorts, tugging them down uselessly, more of a habit than anything now. I really need to stop by the office and grab that order form so I can burn these dang shorts already.

Kristin sees me come through the door and runs over.

"Hey, Hattie!" She smiles; I'm glad for the distraction.

"How's your day going so far?" I ask her. She has her wild hair in French braids, parted in the middle; it looks really cute. My eyes drop down toward her long legs, and I instantly feel sorry for her. The uniform looks even shorter on her.

"I hope your gym partner is more talkative than mine." She nods across the gym in the direction of Josh Campbell, who scowls back at us.

"Wow. What's his deal?" I give him a wide smile and wave enthusiastically. He scrunches up his face and turns his back to us.

"Apparently, he's got something against girls. He thinks being paired with a female for his gym partner is beneath him. I have yet to see his Superman-like athletic abilities." She rolls her eyes. "He did, however, ask me how I can be this tall and female all at once."

"Oh my gosh—how do you even respond to that?" What an absolute tool.

"I just asked him why he wasn't bigger. That shut him up." We both break into laughter just as the bell rings.

"Well, good luck with all that," I say, walking to my spot on the floor.

I look over just as Kellan is taking a seat; he nods in my direction. His dark hair is getting long, and I notice it falling slightly over his forehead. My hands twitch at the thought of brushing it back.

"Okay, class," Coach calls out. "Today, we are doing circuit training. When you hear my whistle, you and your partner will move stations together. There are ten activities and ten sets of partners, so I expect one set per activity at all times. You will notice that there are only nine stations inside the gym; station ten is two laps around the football field. Line up with your partners, and I will assign each pair a starting station. Any questions?"

The class is silent; no one has questions. Even if they do, they don't dare mess with Coach the day before the big game. We can all tell he's tense.

"Excellent!" He blows his whistle, and we hustle into our lines.

———— ♡ ♡ ♡ ————

Kellan and I are group nine, so our first station is sit-ups. Each partner is supposed to hold the other's feet for twenty sit-ups, rotating and repeating as many times as we can before the whistle signals us to change stations.

"You want to go first?" I am dreading the entire idea of this circuit-training plan. I tighten my ponytail and kneel down on the floor.

Kellan sits down across from me and scoots his feet into my hands. "Yeah. I'll show you how it's done if it'll make you feel better." He winks. His white shirt pulls tight across his chest as he stretches his arms behind his head, getting into position. The guy is ridiculously good-looking.

"You really like all this sweaty physical activity, don't you?" I raise a brow as he starts his first sit-up. I watch him breathe in and out. The action seems effortless—up, down, so fluid. I count out loud: one, two, three, four... He's fast and confident in his ability, knocking out his twenty in record time.

When he hits twenty, he lets out a long breath. "I like being physically fit, yeah, but there are much better ways to get sweaty." The dimple in his cheek makes an appearance, and I blush at his words. Was that meant to be an innuendo, or is my mind just in the gutter? Maybe he's talking about football.

I shake my head to clear the words and lie back for my turn. He holds my feet, and I can feel the weight of his hands on my shoes. I place my arms across my chest the way Coach taught me last year and sit up then slowly go back down. My stomach muscles instantly burn, and I struggle through the exercise. Sweat beads across my forehead.

I'm entirely too relieved when Coach's whistle echoes across the gym.

"Well, two laps around the field it is!" I say with mock enthusiasm. At least the company is good—and the view. Kellan leads the way out the doors, and I follow him. But as soon as we are clear of the windows, he takes my hand in his.

"Hattie, I've been wanting to ask you something." I stare at our interlocked fingers and try to catch my breath. The electricity I felt the other day is still there, and it hits me hard. What is happening? My brain is going a million miles a minute, and I'm screaming at it to be quiet. *Pay attention to what he has to say, Hattie. Listen!* I plead with my muddled brain.

"I feel like things have been awkward since school started, maybe even since before the summer ended. There's something different between us. Do you feel that, too?" He hasn't made eye contact with me, which is strange for Kellan—he's always pinning me with those dark eyes, threatening to pull me in.

I'm stunned into silence. He's noticed a change? In me? Great. I've been too flirty, and now he's ready to tell me that our relationship isn't like that. I brace myself for the worst, trying to ignore the heart-sinking panic that is settling over me like a blanket. I heard him and Danny; this is never going to happen.

"I'm not sure what you mean, Kellan," I say cautiously, tucking imaginary loose hairs behind my ear with my free hand.

Finally, he turns to face me, his eyes locking with mine. "If I'm out of line, just say it, but I really want to kiss you, Hattie." My eyes flash to his full lips, and my heart accelerates. *Holy freaking mother-of-pearl! Is he really going to kiss me? Am I about to wake up from a dream?* This is Kellan. Smart, goofy, gorgeous Kellan—and I have never kissed anyone before. What if I don't do it right?

"Hattie?" he asks huskily, leaning his body down to get closer to mine. He lets go of my hand and brings both of his to my face. I can't speak, but I'm afraid if I do nothing, this moment will pass. My skin prickles with goosebumps, and my heart hammers in my ears. I let my eyes fall closed and then eliminate the distance between us.

Our lips brush together, soft as a whisper at first, and I feel the heat of his breath on mine. His lips are even softer than I imagined. His breath smells minty, and his hands slide back to cradle my head, holding my mouth to his. I sigh. He presses in closer, our lips crushing together more frantically. As his fingers weave into my hair, I see stars behind my closed eyes, and suddenly I'm flooded with warmth from my head down through the soles of my feet. I reach out and press my palms against his chest to keep from falling over.

His tongue slides softly over my bottom lip and then ventures into my mouth. The wet heat of it is strange but wonderful. Letting go, I allow myself to explore his mouth with my tongue. Our breathing is quick, our kissing desperate yet sweet. His kiss tastes like stardust and moonlight; I've decided gravity doesn't exist as long as his lips are touching mine.

I let my hands tangle in his hair, my body pressing even closer to him. Despite the height difference, we seem to fit perfectly. His kisses are driving me crazy, and I hear myself moan against his mouth in absolute ecstasy.

Kellan breaks away suddenly, and I stumble back, dazed. My heart leaps into my throat. My face feels flushed, and I struggle to right myself.

"Shit!" His eyes widen. I search his face, but he's back to avoiding eye contact. "I just heard Coach's whistle; I guess we've been out here too long." As if on cue, two of our fellow students push through the gym doors and jog past us. If we don't get a move on, Coach will surely investigate. He runs a tight ship, after all.

I follow a step behind Kellan, trying to catch my breath. Did that kiss not affect him? It absolutely affected me. But he won't look at me—is he already regretting it?

"Kellan?" I ask as we walk into the gym and stop at our next station—medicine ball throwing. I pick up the ten-pound ball and test the weight in my hands. I'm still reeling from that kiss. It was perfect, so much more than I'd imagined a kiss would be. I want to grab his hand and drag him back outside for a second round...

"I'm really sorry. I'm an idiot—I shouldn't have done that." His eyes look pained, and he's slamming the medicine ball too hard against the wall, letting it pelt him when it comes down. I don't know what I did, but I obviously messed this up somehow. He's not thinking about wanting to kiss me again, I can tell—if his body language is any indication, he's trying to erase it from his memory.

My eyes burn, and I focus on throwing the ball against the wall. I can get through the rest of this class without crying—I don't ever cry. I already broke my no-crying rule with Danny this week. I didn't even cry when Mom left us, and I refuse to cry over a boy. Even if that boy is Kellan Anderson, the only boy I've ever truly wanted.

We don't talk again, other than to count push-ups for each other and use whatever limited conversation is needed to get through the remaining stations. Kellan's body is rigid the whole time.

When Coach dismisses us to go to the locker rooms, I sprint to the showers. I need to wash this feeling away. I had my first kiss, an amazingly wonderful kiss, but all I can think about now is the look on Kellan's face when our lips parted. Danny can never find out about this—he won't forgive me for it, and it's not like it will ever happen again. So I turn on the shower and resolve to forget the whole thing ever happened. As if that's even remotely possible.

With the game looming over his head, Danny is distracted at dinner, and I'm relieved. Dad had me order Chinese because he's working late again, so we are sitting at the counter, eating in silence. I try to enjoy the vegetable chow mein that's usually my favorite, but tonight the noodles just taste greasy and sit heavy in my stomach. I push my plate away and stand up from my stool.

"You're not gonna finish that?" Danny asks, looking up from his heaping pile of sweet and sour chicken.

"Nah, I'm not that hungry. You can have it if you want." I push the plate over to him. "I think I'm going to call it a night. Probably just read in bed for awhile." *I kissed your best friend today, and now I feel guilty and sick about it. Oh, and he regrets it, so there's that.* I grimace at my own thoughts.

"Yeah, I'm going to bed soon, too—gotta rest up for the big game." He shovels more chicken into his mouth, and I try not to smile at his enthusiasm.

I briefly consider calling Sam to tell her everything, but I stop myself. I should just let it all go. It's already going to be awkward as hell spending the rest of the semester with Kellan as my gym partner, knowing he regrets our kiss. The kiss that rocked my entire world. The one I can't help but replay over and over in my mind.

I've never kissed anyone before. But something tells me all first kisses aren't that good.

I lie down on my bed and stare at the ceiling, but I don't even see it. I touch my lips with my fingertips, trying to remember exactly how soft Kellan's lips felt on mine, trying to pinpoint the moment when things went wrong for him. Why did he kiss me at all? Why did he stop?

We've been getting closer, and things have been good, haven't they? He's sweet and funny, and he's been opening up to me. The boy that used to protect me during snowball fights and throw me into the pool in the summer is now the boy who will forever be my first kiss. But before I get too far down nostalgic/bliss lane, I remember he's also the constant companion to my brother. And with one stupid-amazing, perfect kiss, I've threatened to ruin that.

"Ugh!" I yell, rolling over and punching my pillow. I might as well just try to sleep.

9

Friday Feels

DANNY DRIVES ME TO school in the morning. Sam is running late, and since she will be coming over after the game anyway, I don't mind the change in routine. Danny's little white car is immaculate. It's nothing like Sam's car, which is filled with sweaters, makeup, hair supplies, old homework, emergency snacks—whatever anyone could possibly need, she's got it stashed in there somewhere.

Danny is drumming his fingers on the steering wheel to the beat of the song on the radio, but I can tell his mind is somewhere else. He always gets quiet before a big game, practicing plays in his head and visualizing a win. Dad taught him that. To visualize the outcome you want, believe it can happen, and then take the steps to get there. I've tried it a few times, but it hasn't seemed to work out that great for me. I must not believe it strongly enough. Or maybe I'm not strong enough to believe it. It takes guts to attempt to manifest something knowing it may never be. It takes strength. A dab of delusion. A heap of hope.

Here's to hoping they win.

I stare out the window as we drive. The leaves are starting to change colors, and the sun is just barely coming up. Fall is here, but it still feels like summer by the afternoon. Part of living in the South, I guess. I want to hold on to these fleeting feelings of summer for as long as they last.

I spent so much time with Danny this summer, worried that it would be our final one together. College is coming for us next year, and as much as I have planned for it, we could end up in separate places. He will go wherever there's a team that wants him. I hate that, knowing he could be all the way across the country from me this time next year.

It's not really a question of *if* a team will want him; scouts were already watching him last year, and Coach says he's going to get offers soon. It's more a matter of *when* and *who*. I depend on him too much, which probably drives him crazy. We've just been a team for our entire existence. We literally came into this world together. We're a package deal—you take one, you get the other.

"What are you thinking about so hard over there?" Danny says, slapping me on the shoulder. I look over at him and realize we've already pulled into the school parking lot—I've been too lost in my thoughts to notice. We're early; only a few cars are scattered around the senior lot. The sun is just peeking through the trees, and the sky is exploding in shades of oranges and pinks beyond the windshield. I take a breath to gather my emotions.

"Just thinking about next year. You know, when you're playing for a college team, and you're too cool to talk to me anymore." I keep my voice light, but I'm only half-joking.

"It's going to be so weird." He's looking at me but running his hands back and forth over the steering wheel. "We've never spent much time apart. Even when we went to summer camp, we went together."

I am touched that he's also thought about this. He's actually afraid to miss me, too. He always seems so independent and carefree as if he doesn't need anyone else in the world but himself. I've envied that about him for most of our lives.

I smile despite the tugging sadness I feel toward the future. "You mean, you're not thrilled to get rid of me and Dad?"

He laughs a little but then turns serious again. "You're annoying, for sure, Hatts, and as for Dad... well, he's Dad. College football has been the ultimate dream for me, and I'm super pumped for it, but I hope you'll be close. We've always been this package deal, but you're going to be using that big brain wherever you end up. You won't miss me."

He's not wrong—we've basically been attached at the hip since we came into this world. The last few years have been more of a subtle attachment. Growing up has, in some ways, caused us to drift a little. We aren't tagging along for each other's dates or anything, but I'm just not ready for any of it to end.

Cars are beginning to fill the spaces around us, but we still have a lot of time before we have to head to class. I don't feel ready to end our conversation just yet. "Danny, do you think if Mom would have stuck around, we'd be as close as we are?" I'm not sure where the question came from, but I am dying to know his answer. Mom keeps popping up in my head lately, and it's bugging the heck out of me. She doesn't deserve my thoughts.

He mulls it over, his forehead creasing in thought as he stares out the front window. "You never ask about Mom. I used to try to get you to talk about her, and you always shot me down." He pins me with a curious look. "I don't really know how different things would be. I'd like to think we were always meant to be this close, though. We have that twin-bond thing, after all." He pats my hand and turns off the idling car. Silence fills the small space, and I want to ask him one more question while I'm feeling brave.

"Would you want to find her, talk to her if you could?" I don't know the answer to that question myself. If you'd asked me a week ago, I would have said "no" in a heartbeat, but my girl hormones are working overtime or something. I'm wondering what things I'm missing in the mother-daughter area of my life. Sam and her mom do all kinds of mother-daughter things, and even though it's never bothered me before, I'm starting to want a mother of my own.

He shakes his head. "I wish I could say no, that I'm not curious about why she left or if she ever regrets her choices. I want to know, though—I want to know why she left Dad. I want to know how she could just walk out and never look back. I want to know if she cried for us like I cried for her." His eyes are wet, and I feel bad for bringing all this up before school—especially on game day.

I ruffle his brown hair like I used to do when we were little, and he gives me a toothy grin. "I'm sorry I got all deep this morning..." I start. "I just know I'm going to miss you. I love you, even though you're a big, annoying jerkface most of the time. I've just been curious about Mom lately, and I hate it. I'm a train wreck." I grab my backpack from between my feet and reach for the door handle. I've given us both enough emotional baggage for one day.

Danny reaches out and stops my hand from opening the door. "Hattie, no matter what, I'll never leave you. Part of me will be with you no matter where I go. You're stuck with my big, annoying jerkface for life, so deal with it." He shoves the door open and pushes me out.

Sam is staring me down across the table at lunch. She knows something is up with me, but I haven't said a single word about what happened. I just want to keep it to myself—is that really too much to ask? Besides, I'm emotionally wrung out from my stupid inquisition about Mom this morning on top of everything else.

"You really expect me to believe you're fine? You haven't had a single bite of your lunch." She pokes at my plate of fries. "Is your dad leaving again? You look like someone ran over your dog."

Dad leaves a lot, so it's a fair question. I do usually get a little melancholy when he goes. We might not be close, but I do love him, and deployments are terrifying. Even if he's a private contractor now, the threats are all still very real over there. He's the only parent we have left; I don't know what Danny and I would do if something actually happened to him.

"No, Dad's not going anywhere that I know of." I force myself to take a few bites of my fries. Usually Fry Friday is my favorite, but I can't seem to muster up any excitement.

The whole school is abuzz today because of the big game tonight, and I know my sour mood sticks out like a sore thumb. Streamers, balloons, and flyers are pinned to every surface. Everyone is chanting the school song and shouting down the hallways. Basically, the entire school looks like the pep squad vomited an entire party store of red and black all over it.

The first game of the season is a huge hookup night, and Sam expects me to be as perky about that as she is. Much to her annoyance, I don't even have the energy to fake it.

She waves her hand in front of my face. "Snap out of it! It's Friday! We have a game to go to, and we are going to find some super-cute boys to talk to and then stuff ourselves with pizza!"

This day really should be exciting—I love game nights, and I have never turned down pizza. I just wish I knew what made Kellan pull away yesterday. And I wish I wasn't so damn afraid to let someone else help me through something for once.

I want to tell Sam everything right now, but I just can't make my mouth form the words. I tell myself it's just easier to deal with things like this alone. "You're right; I'm sorry! We are going to have a great time tonight!" I wipe fry grease from my hands on a napkin.

Sam eyes me for a moment but then grins, clapping her hands together. "Yes!! We are going to look *sooo* good! I'll do your eyeliner in a dramatic wing, and you can help me with my hair!" She sounds excited, and I know I have to pull this one out for her. I can set my feelings aside for a night, can't I?

"We can do a high ponytail with a big bump in front if you want," I suggest. It's one of her favorite hairstyles.

"Ooh! Now you're talking! What did your nana used to say? The higher the hair, the closer to God?" She comes around the table to hug my shoulders. "Welcome back, bestie!"

I don't deserve her.

———— ♡ ♡ ♡ ————

Somehow, I make it through the rest of the day without a permanent scowl on my face. I'm trying to let everything go so I can have fun with Sam tonight.

I will just keep my conversations with Kellan as brief as possible. Maybe if I act like nothing has changed, we can just pretend that kiss never happened yesterday. It's worth a shot, anyway.

I see Kristin in the locker room before gym class, and I smile at the sight of her friendly face. "Hey, girl!" I say, waving as I open my locker. "Ready for sweating hour?"

She laughs and walks over. "Maybe today will be the day Josh stops glaring and becomes my friend."

We both burst into laughter, and I pound my chest, mimicking one of Josh's glares. "You girl, girl bad. Josh no like Kristin."

"Oh my gosh, that's perfect!" Kristin pulls her wild curls back into a ponytail as we change into our gym clothes. "You lucked out in the partner department, huh?"

"Oh, Kellan... yeah, I've known him forever. He's Danny's best friend." *And you best remember that,* I tell myself. *Off-limits, just like you told Sam about Danny.*

"He seems nice." She raises her eyebrows at me, waiting for me to tell her more. I shut my locker and bounce on my toes.

"He's a good guy," I say lamely. I'm a terrible liar—I'm sure my feelings are plastered all over my face. I chew on the inside of my cheek, suddenly anxious about seeing him all over again.

"As I said, I think you won the partner lottery. If you ever want to trade... Josh would probably hate it, and that would make me so happy." Kristin laughs, and it's contagious. We are still laughing when we enter the gym, but the laughter dies when I look up.

I see Kellan leaning on the wall across from the locker room door—it looks like he's been waiting for me. He's wearing jeans and one of those long-sleeved henley shirts that show off his strong arms and lean body. He looks painfully good.

As soon as he sees me, he pushes off the wall and walks over. "Hi, Kristin," he says, nodding at her, and she blushes. "Mind if I borrow my partner for a minute?"

She squeezes my arm, giving me a look that says she knows there is more to our story. She walks away slowly.

"Look, if you just want to forget about yesterday..." I stare at my feet and refuse to look at his face. I might change my mind and try to kiss him again or something if I catch a glimpse of his lips. I'm pathetic.

"Hattie." He tilts my face up, and all the tension and anger from yesterday has left his eyes. His hair is hanging over his forehead just a little, and I hold myself back from brushing it with my fingers. "I don't want to forget. It was dumb, and I shouldn't have kissed you like that. I should have talked to Danny first."

I feel my cheeks heating and clench my hands at my sides. What the heck is he saying? "You don't want to forget?" I chew my lip.

He runs his thumb over my lip, and I release it from my teeth. Goosebumps cover my arms as he leans in close and whispers softly in my ear, "I can't stop thinking about it, about doing it again. But I know Danny won't like it."

I pull back and stare at him. I don't know what to say. Hope blooms in my chest—it *did* affect him as much as it affected me!

He's right about Danny, though—I'm sure of that. He's told us both to back off. This could end badly before it's even started. I blink and cross my arms over my chest, feeling confused and overly exposed talking about this in the gym. Our classmates have started to stare, and the bell is going to ring any minute.

"I have to go do some things for Coach, so I won't be in class. Meet me after the game. I know Danny is going to hate this idea, but I want to see where this goes..." He trails off as the bell interrupts him, and he squeezes my hand gently. "Please say you'll meet me?"

"Okay," I manage, and he turns and walks away while my heart thunders in my ears. This boy is giving me whiplash.

10

Ready? Break!

Friday's game is in full swing by the time Sam and I show up. I'm glad I decided to wear my comfortable shoes since we end up parking almost two blocks away from the field. McKinley Lake might be small, but since football is one of the only forms of entertainment around here, the whole town comes out to watch. So the sorry excuse for a parking lot fills up fast, and most people have to park along the road.

We weren't the only ones who got here far too late for prime parking. Clusters of locals walk beside us toward the field, everyone decked out in Crimson Wolves colors.

At just after seven thirty, the sun has started its descent, but the air is still warm. The ground is still slightly wet from a short Texas downpour an hour ago.

I wanted to look cute tonight, so I curled my long hair. It blows around my face in the breeze—I hope the humidity doesn't make it look like a frizzy mess. My jeans are tight and snug against my legs, and, despite the wind, I wonder if I should have gone with shorts.

"We should have worn fewer clothes!" Sam fans herself and sticks her tongue out. "I mean, we look good, but we are going to sweat out here. I hope someone has a mini fan we can steal." Sam is wearing the same school t-shirt as I am: a solid black tee with crimson-red paw prints and "Go Wolves" printed across the back. Mine says "TATE #12" on the front in honor of my brother. We both decided on blue jeans and Converse. Mine are crimson red, but Sam's are highlighter yellow, and they definitely make a statement.

I pull out my phone and text Danny:

Me: **Just got here. Game start yet?**

Danny: **Warm-up over. Kickoff in 5. Dad here?**

Me: **Not sure. Break a leg.**

Danny: **Not a theater production. Don't want to break anything, thank you very much.**

Me: **W/E. It means GOOD LUCK. Luv U jerkface.**

Danny: **W/E yourself. Luv u 2 punk.**

I stuff the phone back in my pocket.

"I'll get us some frozen lemonade," I say to Sam, walking a little faster. I look for my dad's car as we walk. It's the first game of the season, and he'd promised Danny he'd make it. It's possible I overlooked the car already, but I don't think I did. I really hope he's just running late like me tonight.

The bright field lights buzz, illuminating the twilight sky, and as we get closer to the stands, we are enveloped in the sounds of chatter and whistles. I can hear the cheerleaders in the distance yelling "Go Wolves!"

This is my favorite time of year. I love everything about these football games. The smell in the air. The camaraderie. Even the ringing in my ears from the whistles and cheering that sticks around long after we've all gone home, I find endearing. The energy here is palpable.

I can see a group of kids from our class just inside the gates, and I reach in my pocket for my school ID: our admission inside. We're through the gates almost instantly—being late does have its advantages.

Sam's red hair is pulled back into a ponytail—we made her bump extra-high tonight. Something tells me she needs to be as close to Jesus as she can tonight. Her ponytail swings back and forth as she walks toward the concession stand, quickening her pace. I follow her confident lead.

We get our frozen lemonades and head to the sidelines; I'm thankful to have something cool to hold. I catch Danny's eye from the field, and he raises a hand to blow me an exaggerated kiss. He says he doesn't care if Dad and I come out or not, but I know he watches for us at every game.

Sam watches Danny blow me a kiss, and I wonder if she wishes it was for her. But then she snuggles closer to me as we cradle our cool drinks in our hands, and I shrug off the thought. I'm probably seeing something that isn't there.

I search the field—the team is ready for the kickoff. We are receiving the ball first, which means our team is mostly downfield. But my eyes still find Kellan without any effort—number twenty-four. He always jokes and says he's number twenty-four because he's twice the player Danny is. The truth is, they are both excellent players, and this year's team is rumored to be the one to watch.

The sun has finally disappeared, and now the bright-green turf sparkles under the stadium lights. A sheen of moisture glistens across the artificial turf from the light rain shower earlier—the players will probably slip and slide tonight.

Both sides of the stadium have full sets of bleachers for fans. We are playing the Waco Wildcats, and their royal-blue turnout seems small compared to the sea of crimson and black behind me and Sam. We never sit on the bleachers; we prefer to stand just outside the team area, as close to the action as they'll allow us.

I can't tell if Kellan has noticed that I'm here yet or not, but thinking about our conversation this afternoon makes me nervous all over again. He wants to talk to me alone. I'm almost sick from the anticipation. If he wants us to try to be something, to see where this "thing" leads, all he has to do is ask, and I'm a goner. I know it's crazy and risky, and Danny will probably blow a gasket, but I can't hide my feelings anymore. My lips still buzz when I think about our kiss.

"What are you grinning about?" Sam asks, and I flinch. She's probably been watching me watch Kellan. I feel guilty that I haven't said anything to her yet. She's my best friend, and we don't do secrets. I think about how I'd feel if the tables were turned and she was keeping things from me, and my eyes suddenly prick with moisture. Apparently, I'm hormonal this week. I never cry—the Universe is still playing body-snatcher games with me.

"Sam, if you could set me up with any guy at school, who would you choose?"

Sam's eyes narrow at me, and, for a second, I think she can see straight into my brain. She squeezes my elbow and leans into me, her citrus perfume tickling my nose. "You're into Kellan—you don't notice any other guys." Her voice is soft, and I can't detect any surprise in her tone. I jerk back to search her face.

"You knew?" I say, my response too loud. The air is thick with humidity, and I feel sweat breaking out along my brow. She might not be surprised, but I am. How long has she known that I've had feelings for Kellan? I've only just admitted it to myself this week! "Are you mad I didn't say anything?" I hold my breath.

She's laughing, her lemonade slushing over the side of her cup. She has tears in her eyes. "Am I mad?" She struggles to breathe over her laughter. "If someone doesn't know that you have been crushing on him since the day you met him, they're freakin' blind! Of course I know! I doubt Danny does, though," she adds. "That boy is clueless."

She pulls me into a hug, and I hold my cup to my chest so it won't spill. "Danny is going to kill me, isn't he?" I sigh into her shoulder.

"He'll get over it." She shrugs, backing away a little.

"Why didn't you tell me you knew I liked him?"

"You're so guarded with your feelings—I figured you'd tell me when you were ready." This is why she's my best friend. She just gets me. "But since you're coming clean now, do tell! What's new in the land of Kellan?" She grins.

"He wants to talk to me after the game." Telling Sam my secret feels liberating. I don't know why I waited. Even if she thinks I'm a hypocrite after this, she loves me. I feel the first tinges of hope that this might all work out.

"Danny?" She's turned toward the field now, and I feel like she isn't listening to me at all, which is odd. She lives for juicy gossip, and I am handing her a fresh-squeezed glass.

"No, I'm talking about Kellan. He asked me to meet him after the game. He said he wants to talk to me about something." I stare at my feet, waiting for her to respond, but she doesn't. A hush breaks out over the stands, and then I notice a commotion out on the field. I glance up, and the grass is flooded with players and coaches. I've clearly missed something. Something big.

$$\text{———} \ \heartsuit \ \heartsuit \ \heartsuit \ \text{———}$$

"CALL 9-1-1!!! SOMEONE BRING THE AED!" Coach Black is yelling as he rushes toward the huddle of players.

Someone must be hurt. I snap to attention, scanning the turf for the two silhouettes I know by heart.

"Hattie, I think Danny's hurt!" I hear Sam say, but I'm already sprinting out onto the field. I push past the massive bodies of red and blue, shoving my way through the players to get to the huddle.

Danny is on the ground, his face toward the sky, but I can't see his eyes. The coaches are yelling, but I can't hear the words over the piercing sound of nothingness in my ears. It's deafeningly loud. Coach Black is trying to get Danny's pads and helmet off; I don't understand what's happening. He's so still—the whole thing doesn't look right.

"Back up, everyone—give us some space!" Coach Black yells, his voice booming, his eyes black as night. The players around me step back, but I'm frozen in place, just out of reach. I watch as Kellan removes Danny's helmet. His eyes are closed; he's unconscious, and the fear in me mounts, threatening to level me. Someone is cutting through his crimson jersey, right down the middle between the solid black number twelve. They're ripping it in their haste to get it off, pulling frantically at pads and wiping his chest down with towels. They've shoved a blanket underneath his body to get him off the wet ground. His chest is no longer heaving in that strange pattern. He's gone much too still.

Coach starts doing compressions. I count with him: one, two, three, four, five, six, seven, eight... I look at Danny's face again. No change—he's too still. I'm frozen there, horrified and unable to look away. I sink to my knees on the turf; I find his fingers and squeeze. *Please, Danny.*

They attach the two medical pads to his chest as Coach continues CPR, and the AED machine's robotic voice starts giving them step-by-step instructions. When it tells everyone to stand clear, Kellan places his hand on my arm, and I reluctantly let Danny's fingers drop to his side. "Shock will be delivered in, three, two, one. Shock." Danny's body jerks and then goes still.

The machine speaks again. "You may now touch the patient. Continue CPR."

Coach immediately goes back to pumping his chest. Thirty compressions, one breath, a pause for the machine to check for a pulse and another shock.

I stare at the face of the person I love most in this world and beg God to do something. I can hear someone yelling, "OH GOD, OH GOD, OH MY GOD." I wish they'd shut up. I wish he'd wake up. I wish for anything but this.

———— ♡ ♡ ♡ ————

Time is passing, but I don't know how long I have been kneeling, helplessly watching. Maybe an hour has passed or maybe it's only been a few minutes.

At some point, though, I'm sure. Maybe it was the way Coach's compressions slowed. The way some of Danny's teammates began to cry. I'm not sure. But I know without a doubt, my brother is dead. I can almost see his soul leaving his body. Not like a ghost, not like some big production, but somehow his body suddenly loses its light. He looks like a shell now, missing the magic that makes us who we are. The life force, the spark—the thing that separates the living from the dead.

I recognize from the rawness in my throat, realize that those strangled cries I'd heard calling out for God moments ago were my own. My knees are numb from the wetness that has seeped through my jeans. Everything's cold. Everything's numb.

Making myself move now feels impossible. I continue to stare at the face of the body that used to be Danny. Warm tears burn tracks down my cheeks, the wind smearing them across my face. I watch as the paramedics arrive; Coach calls out to them as they scramble around him. I listen as he informs them of the steps they've taken.

"It's been twenty minutes, and we haven't been able to get him back."

"We'll take over from here." One of the paramedics steps in to replace Coach, who crumples to the ground. They try to shock his heart, they continue administering CPR, but I can tell they're only doing this for us. They already know the truth: It's too late for Danny.

Since before we even came into the world, we have existed together. It's like we've shared one soul split between two bodies. He's part of me in a way that no one else can ever be. Only now, the Universe is wrong somehow. His half of our soul has left his body, and I don't know how to process any of it. I don't know how to exist without half of my soul.

They've worked diligently on my brother for awhile now. The stands have been emptied, the field cleared. And the paramedics eventually admit defeat. I hear someone say the coroner is on his way, that someone official has to declare the time of death, that it's a legality. *It's been too long—there's no hope left.* They all occasionally toss a concerned look my way, but I don't move; I just can't. Once I move from this place, will I ever see him again? Even if it is just his body, I want to hold on to whatever is left of him for as long as they'll allow it.

Once they stopped shocking him, I'd grabbed his hand. I'm still holding it in mine, but it feels colder with each passing minute. I wish I could move closer, wish I could pound my hands on his chest and beg him not to leave me. He promised me he wouldn't. I want to shake him. *Danny! Danny, how could you? You can't leave me!*

I love you.

I feel a hand on my shoulder from behind, but I don't have it in me to turn around. I stay frozen, eyes on Danny, praying I'll just wake up from this nightmare.

"Hattie?" The voice is choked and raw—it belongs to Kellan. He comes around and kneels on the ground with me. His arms wrap around me tightly. I don't think he's ever left my side. "Hattie, do you need me to call your dad?" he asks quietly. Dad. How will Dad deal with this? Why the hell isn't he here? He's never around when we need him. He's never around even when we don't. He will never see Danny alive again—neither of us will.

I feel like I'm going to be sick—my body shakes violently, and my teeth chatter uncontrollably. I don't answer Kellan. I want to, but I don't want to.

Everything is wrong.

The ground spins beneath me. If I wasn't already on my knees, I'd probably fall over. I press my palms against Kellan's chest and try to breathe.

Kellan shifts in his heavy pads, tilting my face up so he can look me in the eye. His eyes and face are red and streaked with tears. He takes my face in his hands—they're warm against my cheeks—and, despite the temperature outside, my body feels ice cold. His thumbs brush at the wetness on my face, and his lip trembles. "Hattie, talk to me, please."

My eyes blur with more tears, and his tortured face swims in the haze. I don't know how to speak around the ball of emotion lodged in my throat. I should ask him to call my dad. Even if he isn't the best dad, he should be here. He will know what to do next. Even in my weak and anxious state, I know I need him now. I try to nod, but it's jerky and awkward. I try to speak, but only a strangled cry escapes my lips. I'm completely broken.

"Please." It's barely a whisper, but he hears me. He nods once, briskly swiping at his eyes before pressing a kiss to my forehead. Then he slowly stands and walks away from me to make the call. I don't hear the words he says to my dad, but I don't have to. It doesn't matter what words he chooses, because they all amount to the same thing.

My brother is gone.

11

In the Aftermath

EVERY TIME I TRY to speak, my throat fills up with cement. The burning in my eyes remains constant, invisible needles permanently lodged in each eyeball. My tongue feels swollen and much too big for my mouth.

It doesn't matter, anyway. I have no words worth vocalizing. The only thought in my head keeps repeating like a skipping song.

He's gone. I'm alone.

He's gone. I'm alone.

He's gone.

I'm alone.

I am alone.

Somehow, I wake up in my own bed, but I don't remember how I got there. I curl up into a ball—into myself—under the blankets and cry. Silent, tearless gasps for air wrack my body. My entire world has ended, and I don't have a single ounce of fight left in my bones. I'm a shell of what I used to be, replaced by despair and turmoil. There is nothing else.

After the first night without him, I lost track of time. I'm not sure if I slept. I just remember wishing for death to take me—sleep wasn't what I wanted. I watched the sun rise and set and rise again, or at least I think I did. I was unmoving, but no one bothered me. My blankets were pulled up around me, the familiar smells and sounds of home nipping at my consciousness. I only felt numb.

Home.

It would never be home again.

Danny was my home.

———— ♡ ♡ ♡ ————

I wake to someone shaking my shoulder, and in my half-awake state, I cry out, "Danny?"

"No, honey, it's me, Uncle Dan," he says softly, patting my arm. "Your dad said you haven't come out of your room for two days. He said he tried to talk to you a few times, but you told him to go away, and he doesn't want to upset you more."

In my mind, that was just a dream, yelling at Dad that he should leave because he's never there when we need him anyway. I wince at the thought. He didn't deserve that, but the anger still throbs in my veins.

I feel so out of control. My head is aching, and I'm sure my eyes are swollen from crying so much. I feel numb this morning. Well, I think it's morning. Light is streaming through the windows as I sit up slowly.

"How are you here?" My voice is barely a whisper, raspy and raw, and my throat feels like I've swallowed glass. I look at Uncle Dan—his large, muscled body is dressed in cargo pants and a black t-shirt. I feel nothing. Not the normal comfort nor the rush of familiarity. Just nothing.

He hands me a glass of water, and I take a timid sip.

"I caught the first flight out of Kuwait when I heard..." He trails off, swallowing hard. I watch his Adam's apple rise and fall. "I'm sorry I wasn't here."

I shake my head. What difference would it have made? Coach and the paramedics did everything they could to save Danny. If there had been any chance, we wouldn't be having this conversation.

Uncle Dan and Dad have both buried so many of their soldiers over the years. Danny and I even knew some of them: young men, mostly. Their mothers had come and cried as they folded flags and fired shots into the air. Each one took a little piece of Dad away from us.

There would never be an "us" again. I recoil at the thought. I feel shell-shocked, and I just keep waiting for someone to tell me it's all been a dream. I know it's not, though. I'm no stranger to the harsh realities of life. I'm always being left behind.

I push my wild hair out of my face and look up. "What do I do now?" I need someone to tell me how to breathe, how to process. I'm failing miserably. I just want to close my eyes and cease to exist.

Uncle Dan runs a hand over his stubbled jaw—it's weird to see the strawberry-blonde whiskers on his face.

He's always clean-shaven, the picture of discipline. But now, even the matching hair on the top of his head looks disheveled. It's barely long enough to do anything, but it looks pressed down in strange places. Dark circles under his bloodshot eyes and creased lines in his forehead tell a story of weariness that I feel mirrored in my bones. This isn't the way it's supposed to go.

"There will be a funeral a week from Friday. They insisted on an autopsy because of his age, so that is causing a slight delay. He died from sudden cardiac arrest—they think he probably had an undiagnosed heart defect..." His voice cracks, tears threatening to fall from his eyes should he even blink, and I look away from him. I don't really want to hear any of this. I don't want to know the details; I just want it all to be a misunderstanding. I want to go next door and find Danny in his bed, hear him break down everyone's performance from Friday's game the way we've done after every game he's played since we've lived here.

My hand trembles as I set the half-empty cup of water on the nightstand beside me. Uncle Dan is still staring at me with unveiled concern on his face. "What day is it?" I ask. What I really mean is "how long have I been out of it?" I know I don't have to say that, though. Uncle Dan has always had a way of reading me.

"It's Sunday afternoon; it's been two days." He reaches out and takes my hand. "Hattie, this is probably going to be the hardest thing you've ever done. I'm not going to lie—it's going to suck. It's going to take all the strength you have in you to get through this week and the week after that for a long while. But promise me you'll reach out if

you need one of us. We love you. Me, Melissa, your dad...
we just want to help you in any way we can."

I look down at our hands. His are scratchy and scarred
like my dad's. One of his hands completely engulfs my
smaller one. I wish the world would swallow me up just
like his palm is doing. "I should probably go to school
tomorrow," I say.

"Hattie, I don't think so." He winces. "A shower,
maybe? Some food?"

My stomach lurches at the mention of food. I know
there's nothing in my stomach, but I feel like I could vomit
something up. I shake my head hard, swallowing back the
urge. "No, I can't eat."

"A shower then? And maybe call one of your friends?
Sam has called a few times—Kellan, too." I close my eyes.
He's right. I can't go to school—I'm not ready to face
anyone. I'm not even ready to talk to anyone. But a shower
might be good. At least if I cry in there, the water will take
my tears and give my pillowcase a break.

"Okay, I'll take a shower and maybe some green tea?"
I say this more to give Uncle Dan something to do than
anything else. Still the peacekeeper.

"Sure. I'll make some toast, too, just in case you change
your mind about eating."

Smiling weakly, I climb out of bed. My legs are shaky,
and my head pounds like a base drum. I'm still wearing my
clothes from the game, my knees stained from kneeling on
the turf. As I step into the bathroom, I study the marks.
The door to Danny's room is closed, and I'm thankful—I
don't know how I'll ever go in there again.

I brace my hands on both sides of the sink and brave a look at myself in the mirror.

Two black, smeared, puffy eyes glare back at me, eyes that are red and swollen behind the mascara that has melted down my cheeks, giving them ghostly rings. My hair is a huge mass, wild and tangled, and my lips are dry and cracked. I look horrifying, and I don't even care.

I stare at the toothbrush holder on the counter, at Danny's toothbrush in the slot next to mine. His electric razor sits on the charging dock, and his cologne bottle is perfectly centered on his side of the sink. I feel tears burning at the back of my throat. He's everywhere. He's everywhere, and he's nowhere.

I open the top drawer and shove everything inside, my chest heaving. Just Friday morning, he promised he would never leave me. He promised, and a whole lot of good that did.

12

D is for Denial

I EASILY AVOIDED DAD that first week, especially with Uncle Dan and Melissa rushing around and making noise in the house. Our house is big so that we can accommodate a revolving door of transitioning soldiers. Normally, the soldiers stay in the extra rooms downstairs and only come up to use the kitchen—our family bedrooms are all upstairs, which affords us a little more privacy.

Uncle Dan is family, so he and Melissa chose a room upstairs, and I could not escape their presence. But I tried—I didn't leave my room at all. I refused to do anything more than lie in my bed.

People dropped by periodically with casseroles and other frozen food items for meals, all of which I wouldn't eat. The most Uncle Dan could get into me was a bite or two of toast on occasion with a sip of green tea for show. My stomach couldn't stand the idea of anything more substantial.

I watch the days tick by on my digital clock. It's been ten days now since Danny's game.

Any time I hear the phone ringing or someone at the front door, I lock myself in my room and turn out the lights. If I can just stay hidden in here, I might be able to avoid all the sympathetic looks and words that I don't care to receive.

I've heard talk that today, some more of Dad's old soldiers will be arriving and crashing in the house until the funeral on Friday. I hope everyone has the sense to keep them out of Danny's room—other than the kitchen, they have no business being on this floor.

I'm trying to work up the nerve to go in and lock Danny's door from the inside. So far, I've only gone into our connecting bathroom a few times and then turned around. One time, I actually reached for the door handle, but I snatched my hand back as if I had been burned before I even made contact. The fish on our shower curtain mocked me with their little eyes.

I turned my cell phone off without looking at any of the messages. I kind of wonder where Danny's phone is right now and if it's also going crazy. The house phone, which only a handful of people actually have the number to, has been ringing off the hook. Before all this, it barely rang at all. If it did, the calls were always spam callers from overseas saying our computers were under attack. Danny liked to put on fake accents and mess with them.

No matter how hard I try, all my thoughts lead back to Danny.

The phone rings again, and irritation starts to bubble in my veins. I pick the phone up and slam it back into its cradle. Take that, obnoxious person. They'll probably call back again. I know Melissa has been answering the phones and accepting things from people at the door. It's really nice of her, but I kind of wish she'd just tell them all to go home and leave us alone. What sick satisfaction do they get out of coming over here to see us at our worst? Don't they know we're drowning? Don't they think it would be better to just see us at the funeral?

My stomach lurches hard, and I rush for the toilet, knees bruising on the tile as I hurl the contents of my stomach into the bowl. The funeral. Uncle Dan had mentioned something to me this morning over my three diligent bites of toast that have now been flushed down the pipes. I need to choose a dress to wear for the service, and he wondered if I would be willing to go through Danny's clothes and choose his final outfit. He didn't want to press me, but it's Tuesday, and the funeral director needs the clothes by Thursday afternoon.

Final outfits. I've known that's a thing for a very long time. I've been to a few funerals, the most recent one for our nana a few years back. She had an open casket funeral, too, and someone had put her in a yellow sundress with a thick white collar that looked like an absolutely ridiculous thing for a dead person to wear. Maybe Dad had chosen it—I never asked. The dress looked like something a five-year-old would proudly wear to meet the Easter Bunny, and Nana's cheeks were much too pink from the makeup they used, which only made it worse.

Danny and I got into trouble for giggling about it in the pews during her service. We came up with a funny story about how Nana had been such a good girl that she got to go back to the land of children, and the Easter Bunny would be here to get her any minute. Dad didn't hear what we were saying, but he shushed us with a murderous look in his eyes. I remember Kellan's mom rushing over to sit between us, placing our hands in her lap and smiling kindly at us.

Kellan. I haven't let my mind go there since the game on Friday night. He called Dad, dealt with the questions from the paramedics because I was absolutely useless, and then he drove me home from the field.

It's still kind of fuzzy in my mind. I remember him gently placing me in his truck. Had he carried me from the field? I remember him reaching over me and buckling my seatbelt and saying something about how sorry he was. Did I say anything back? I don't remember the drive or how I got into the house. I think Dad was here, but I can't remember.

I slide to the floor against the footboard of my bed. I throw my head back, letting it crack against the wood over and over until it hurts. I'm curious if I can feel any more pain than I already do. It's strange to feel so numb inside while simultaneously engulfed with pain. It shouldn't be possible, and yet, that's exactly how it feels.

Deep down, I know that no one is to blame for what happened to Danny. I'm smart enough to know that sometimes these things remain a medical mystery. One of those bad things that happen to good people.

I can't help but feel immense guilt over our last moments together. The last few days and weeks of inappropriate thoughts about his best friend. The sneaking around, that kiss. I am going to have to live with knowing that when my brother died, I was lying to him.

Okay, maybe I wasn't lying flat out, but lying by omission is the same, isn't it? I throw my head back again, and my teeth hit my tongue. I taste blood, which makes me feel slightly better. I deserve to hurt.

I don't know how I'm supposed to face Kellan. I don't even know what he's feeling or thinking. Maybe he's got this guilt clawing at him from the inside, too, eating him alive.

Maybe he won't ever want to speak to me again. Danny was his best friend; they were practically brothers. I was just the twin sister who he thought was cute. I'm sure he'd rather get me out of his system and move on with his life. It was inevitable—graduation would have separated us, anyway.

If the earth could just swallow me up whole soon, I'd appreciate it.

I shake my head. I have tasks to complete, for God's sake! I need to focus. What do you wear to the funeral of the person you love the most? What would Danny want to wear? Not a tux, that's for sure. He has the one he wore to Junior Prom last fall tucked in the back of his closet—he'd called it his "obligatory monkey suit." I know it would probably be the ideal thing for him to wear; it's what people would be expecting, right? To see him dressed up smartly as he lay in that box?

Chills come over me thinking about how he will look in there. Like he looked on the field. As if his body is a shell missing all the things inside that make it definable. Like a stuffed animal without all its stuffing, sort of how it was intended but wrong. A candle whose wick has been removed, a coffee mug that someone snapped the handle off of: It still seems relatively correct, but a trained eye would spot the difference immediately. It's Danny's shell, but it's not Danny.

I hear the doorbell, and I groan audibly. Why can't these people just go away?

I use the frustration and irritation I'm feeling to fuel my movements. I push off the floor and onto my feet, clad in light-purple socks. I've taken to wearing the clothes in the back of my drawer to avoid leaving my room. I'm not ready to retrieve the huge pile of laundry waiting for me in the laundry room, because my clothes won't be the only ones in there. Seeing Danny's pile might destroy me.

I have on a pair of gray sweatpants that are a size too small and an oversized black t-shirt that falls off my shoulder every time I move. I think I stole it from Dad to use as pajamas last summer.

I stare at the purple socks as I take each step. Left foot, right foot, left foot... and then I'm standing in our shared bathroom. I'm right in front of the door to Danny's room. I flex my fingers as if that will give them the strength to take that final step. I close my eyes, hold my breath, and turn the handle.

I throw open the door before I can change my mind, and just as it slams against the wall on the other side, I open my eyes and let out a bloodcurdling scream.

13

An Unexpected Visitor

"Danny?!" I scream, rushing toward the hunched body on the floor. But as soon as I make contact, I instantly realize my mistake. From his hooded back they look similar, but the feel of him is wrong. It's not Danny at all, and his body is shaking and moaning in pain. The sounds coming from him resemble the cries of a helpless wounded animal.

It's Kellan, and the second I make the connection, my heart is in my throat. I'm filled with rage and something else I can't define, but I recognize the unmistakable urge to comfort him.

I get in front of him; his crimson hoodie is wrinkled, and I smooth my hands over his shoulders, pushing him into a sitting position. I want to see his face, even though I know it's going to hurt. Everything hurts—what's one more thing on the pile? Sunlight floods the room so there's no need to turn on the lights.

"Kellan, look at me," I say quietly. His face shoots up, his eyes locking on mine as if he's just realizing I'm here. I don't know how my screaming didn't alert him before.

"Hattie?" I don't think it's really a question. His eyes inventory my face and body and then return to mine as his hands reach up to circle my wrists that rest on his shoulders, holding them still. His fingers feel ice-cold against my skin, but I welcome them—I need to feel something piercing to prove I'm still alive. "I've been calling, and I've come by a few times..." The pain in the gravel of his voice is great, and my heart lurches. I don't want to cry again. I'm terrified that the next time I start crying, I won't be able to stop.

"How did you get inside?" I ask. I remember hearing the doorbell ring, but I didn't hear anyone come down our hallway.

"I kept coming by, but Melissa kept turning me away at the door. She said no one was ready for guests." His voice breaks on a sob. "Hattie, I needed to see you. I needed to feel Danny again. I needed to come here and be close to him. I know that probably sounds weird, but it's the only place I want to be." He looks ashamed, so vulnerable, and absolutely broken.

My anger subsides, so I nod, encouraging him to keep talking.

"I used the ladder we use when we miss curfew and climbed in the window. We broke the lock a few years ago so I knew I could get in."

"You came in through the window?" I don't trust myself to say anything substantial, so I just repeat his words back to him. I pull free of his hands and join him on the floor, sitting cross-legged in front of him.

"It was stupid, right? I know I should have waited like Melissa asked me to. I was just going to stay a second, but as soon as I got inside..." Tears stream from his eyes, and I watch them make tracks down his reddened cheeks. It's the only color on his face—otherwise, he's as pale and disheveled as I've been all week.

"I get it," I nod, but only to offer him some comfort. I don't dare look around or breathe too deeply. I haven't let the shock of seeing him in Danny's room subside. I'm thankful for the surprise, for this distraction, regardless of how it makes me feel to be in Danny's room with Kellan and not Danny. I reach out and touch Kellan's wet cheek with my palm, and his eyes close as he leans into my touch. His face is rough against my skin—he hasn't shaved. I like the way it feels.

"I was so worried about you." He sighs, and I suddenly feel guilty for my silence. I'm surprised I can feel anything at all. Ten days of silence, ten days of absolute hell. I never thought Kellan would need me—I hadn't let myself go there.

There's a knock at the door. "Hattie? Is everything alright in there? We heard a scream..." Uncle Dan's voice sounds muffled, but I can hear the concern etched in it.

"Everything is fine. I'm sorry I screamed," I say, scrambling. I don't want anyone to see Kellan here. As much as I don't stand behind his breaking and entering, I'm not ready for anyone to kick him out. And maybe they wouldn't, but I'm not willing to take that chance. I stand, walk over to the door, and open it just enough to see Uncle

Dan's face. "I just need a few minutes. I'm trying to work up the nerve to open Danny's closet."

"Take your time. We just heard the scream and wanted to make sure you were okay." He puts his hands up and looks down the hallway. "There's dinner if you feel like eating."

"I think I'll take some to my room tonight, thanks." I give him a weak smile in an attempt to sell the lie.

He smiles back. "Wonderful. I'll tell Melissa to put a plate in the microwave for you." He turns away, and I quickly shut and lock the door. Then I take a deep breath and turn back to face Kellan.

"Thanks for not ratting me out," he says softly, wiping his eyes. I'm relieved to see him standing on his feet. I'm not used to seeing all of the strong men in my life crumbling before me—everything in my world feels like it has shifted in an unnatural way. "I can leave if you really want me to go. I know we left things weird before everything went to shit." He shifts from one foot to the other, and I'm caught off guard by this vulnerable side of him. He's always been so confident, so sure of himself.

"I have to pick out Danny's last outfit." I swallow hard around the growing lump in my throat and motion to the closet doors. "I don't want to do this alone; will you help me? I doubt anyone knew him better than you."

Kellan stops shifting and pulls his hood off his head. His dark hair is falling over his forehead like it always does, and he clenches his jaw, his eyes searching for something in mine. I bite my lip nervously, wondering what's going on in his head. I don't have to wonder long.

His eyes flash, and he stalks toward me—I hold my breath, frozen in place by his gaze. Before I can protest, his body is pressed against mine, and his hands slide over my jaw then get lost in my hair. I taste the salty tears that linger as his soft lips crash into mine.

As I wrap my arms around his neck, standing to my full height and pulling him even closer, I feel warm for the first time in days. I let my fingers intertwine with the soft hair at the back of his head and breathe him in. Despite his disheveled appearance, he smells clean. His cologne is barely hanging onto his clothes, and I get a subtle whiff of his body wash.

Our kiss deepens, and Kellan's hands come down around my shoulders, holding me to him. I can feel his heart beating wildly against mine, so I let myself completely surrender to his kiss. It's a stolen moment of calm in our chaos, and, for just a moment, I allow myself to feel security in his arms.

The doorbell rings again, and my mind begins to clear. We're in Danny's room, and we are kissing. Shame rushes over my body, engulfing me in its thick fog. I push back, out of his embrace, and clap a hand over my mouth. What am I doing?

"What is it?" Kellan asks, reaching for me. I dodge his grasp and stare at the ceiling as if I'll find the answers I'm looking for up there. I suddenly feel like I'm going to be sick again. I've spent days feeling guilty for lying to Danny, and now here I am right back at it? And in his room...

"I can't do this. Danny would hate this so much." I gesture between us, my stomach rolling, my heart and my mind each demanding something else from me. Being in his arms felt so right, but I know I'll just beat myself up for it later. I have to end this now before either of us does something we can't take back.

"I need to pick out an outfit for Danny, and then I think you should go." I hope he can't hear the lie in my voice. I do want him to go, but I also want him to stay. I'm a walking contradiction.

Kellan's face falls along with his outstretched hand. He balls both fists at his sides and nods. "I'll help."

I know he wants to say something else, anything else to avoid swallowing the fact that I've just kicked him out of my house after he put himself out there again, but he doesn't. We both walk toward the closet without speaking another word.

Danny's walk-in closet is immaculately organized; even the hangers are equally spaced. You could check them with a ruler and I'm positive the spacing would be exact. This is the only part of his room where I've never really had a chance to roam. He was always secretive about his closet, and I never pressed him. I didn't want him touching my books, and he didn't want me in his closet; we had a mutual understanding.

I feel equal parts anxiety and curiosity as I touch each piece of clothing. It smells just like Danny in here, a mixture of sandalwood and citrus, and I feel comforted by the familiar smell. I hug one of his shirt sleeves to my face for just a moment.

I see his dress clothes against the back: slacks he wore to football banquets and church functions Nana dragged us to and a handful of button-up collared shirts in varying shades of blue and black. Tucked against the wall at the end hangs his suit from last year's Junior Prom.

"None of this seems right." I gesture at the hanging dress clothes. I know he would hate all of these options.

Kellan nods at me. I think he knows what I mean—he hasn't said a word since we stepped into the closet. His hands are still fisted at his sides, and he seems to be shaking a little. I push down the guilty feelings.

"It won't be right no matter what you choose." Kellan finally speaks. "He shouldn't be dead. It's all wrong." His eyes turn hard, his sadness gone for a moment and replaced with hostility. He reaches up to the shelf above the hanging clothes and grabs a football, pressing it hard between his palms.

I watch him closely; his body shakes as he seems to gather his thoughts.

"I don't understand any of it. He was fine. He was fine before the game—we were laughing and joking about kicking the crap out of Waco... He was going to ask Sarah to come to pizza with us after the game..." He shifts the ball back and forth between his hands, shaking his head. He looks like he's somewhere else. I want to reach out and touch him, let him know I'm still here with him, but I hold back. I don't want to give him the wrong idea. I don't know if I have the willpower to stop touching him if I let myself start.

"He'll never get to play football in college or go for the pros. He could have made it, too. He was good at everything. He deserved to live. It's not fair! It's all shit!" He throws the ball hard, and it hits low on the back wall and ricochets into a stack of notebooks. They spew out into the closet. His eyes go wide, and his body buckles as he collapses to his knees. "Oh God, I'm such an idiot!"

I watch him scramble to right the stack of notebooks; I see the stress on his face. I should be concerned that he's upset the balance of Danny's closet, the one untouched spot my brother left behind, but instead, my heart is breaking for him. He's lost something precious, too.

I've been feeling so sorry for myself. Yes, I lost Danny, my brother, but I am not the only one who loved him. He was so easy to love. My resolve crumbles a little, and I place my hand on Kellan's shoulder.

"It *is* all shit." I fall to my knees beside him. "Don't worry about this mess—I'll clean it up later." Breaking my own rules, I take his hands in mine and really look at him. His thick lashes flutter lightly as he stares at our hands. He's such a beautiful boy, just like my brother—they were the most beautiful pair of boys, inside and out. I thought I'd spend the rest of my life watching the two of them together.

"I need to go to the kitchen before Uncle Dan or Melissa comes looking for me. I don't know how to do any of this; I don't know how I'm going to feel from one second to the next. Just do me a favor?" I hold my breath, and he finally looks up at me.

"Anything," he whispers, and I know he means it.

"Bring me his extra football jersey from school? I think that's what he should wear."

Kellan gives me one of his real smiles, his dimple flashing. "Hell yes, he would love that."

14

To Read or Not to Read

IT'S THURSDAY MORNING, AND I haven't talked to anyone since Tuesday when I found Kellan in Danny's room. I've been stuck in a state of in-between, hoping Kellan would drop in again and praying that he wouldn't. His mom stopped by yesterday and dropped off a frozen meal and some banana bread. Tucked in the bottom of the paper bag was Danny's extra jersey, and I silently thanked Kellan for pulling through.

I took the jersey into my room and tucked it under my pillow. I'd spent the night holding it against my chest and breathing, trying to feel as close to Danny as I could, trying to imagine what he'd be saying or doing now. I know how much he'd hate all this fuss over him. Danny lived for two things: spreading happiness and football.

He would be really disappointed in my efforts with Dad.

Danny was always good at bridging the gap between me and Dad. I know I'm being cruel, but I still haven't seen him. I've avoided him with the stealth of a practiced veteran. He isn't going to push, and I'm not going to budge.

Uncle Dan has given me a few well-placed talks about sticking together in times of tragedy, but I shut him up quickly each time with a few bites of soup or by asking for more tea. Melissa never bothers me—she breezes out of the room whenever I enter. I have the sneaking suspicion she feels like an intruder in our house. She doesn't know us that well; she isn't quite part of the family yet.

Danny would tell me to give Dad a break, but I just keep seeing them together at the sink Friday morning, side by side, practically twins in all their features. I'm afraid that when I finally set my eyes on Dad, it'll be too much. I'll see his eyes, Danny's eyes, and it'll break me. I'm already kind of broken, but I'm holding the little pieces together with as much grit and determination as I can muster.

I go to Danny's room and step into his closet. It still has his smell, even though Kellan and I disturbed the peace with our presence just two days ago. I tug his favorite pair of jeans off the hanger, the ones with a hole on each knee and a small red stain on the back from wiping spirit paint on them.

He was seeing Kayla at the time of the stained jeans. She was super into all things spirit related, a flyer on the cheerleading team. He spent so many weekends painting signs with her for fundraisers, and he even helped her build a float for the homecoming parade.

They made a really cute couple. She was tall and blonde, which was typically Danny's type. She was also bubbly and sweet, and I really liked her a lot. He'd taken her to Prom last year, and I'm pretty sure he lost his virginity to her that night, too. Not that he was the type to tell anyone something so personal. He didn't kiss and tell, and not because that was considered bragging, but because he was a true gentleman.

I think he might have loved Kayla, or could have. She moved away over the summer, though. Her dad got a job in Tennessee or something like that, and they just decided it would be easier to break up before she left. He seemed a little dejected for a week or so, and then it was like she had never been his girlfriend at all. He put her pictures away and went back to being the same old wild Danny.

Sometimes, I find myself wondering if Danny and I are broken. We've always loved each other, and we love Dad and Uncle Dan, but I'm not sure we're capable of loving anyone else, anyone that's not family.

Even being family isn't enough to warrant our love. I don't feel any love when I think about my mother. I think we've loved and lost too many people to trust that it's worth the risk, so we just hold back. We don't let anyone get close enough to hurt us.

A lot of good that did me. Danny is gone, and he's the one person I thought would never leave me, the one person I allowed myself to love without any reservations. I love my dad, too—don't get me wrong. It's just that Dad seems like he could disappear from my life at any moment, and that's on a good day. I've never trusted that he is here permanently. He leaves us all the time, and I'm not always sure that the job demands he goes as often as he does—I think he goes because he needs to. Something in Dad is just as broken as whatever is broken with Danny and me. Some kind of unfortunate genetic trait.

Maybe we were always going to be broken. With two broken parents, how are the children supposed to come through unscathed? *Not enough love in this house,* Nana had said. What kind of damage could that do? I stare at the jeans in my hands, tracing my fingers over the red paint stain, the last evidence of Kayla's brief time in Danny's life. I wonder if she'll cry when she hears about him. If I ever find the courage to log on to social media, I'm sure I'll see posts on Facebook and comments on Instagram by now. Eventually, I'll have to look, but for now, I am content to stay in the dark.

I sit down on the floor, folding my legs underneath me, clutching the jeans tightly to my chest. I know Danny has a pair of red Converse in the back of his closet somewhere, and I start to move the toppled notebooks out of the way. One notebook is lying open, and his handwriting catches my eye. I set the jeans aside and pick the notebook up to examine it.

Darkness explodes into light
Day is born from the night
and still I wait
Flames engulfing all they touch
The fire inside me is burning too much
and still I wait
Buildings crumble, cities fall
I shouldn't have waited this long to call
and now you're done waiting
and now you're really gone

Danny always carried a notebook in his backpack. He'd write through dinner sometimes or in his room quietly, hiding out for hours. I always wondered what he was writing in those notebooks. Football plays, comic strips, to-do lists—he was always so secretive about it. If I'd known it was poetry, journals, whatever this is, I definitely would have teased him. Now, though, I have a piece of his heart, his mind, that I can hold in my hands. I flip quickly to the next page, eager for more of his words.

She makes me so mad. She's always doing things she knows will get under my skin. It's like she's purposely trying to make me crazy. Dad said I should just be nice, that these years are hard for teenage girls. How the heck does he know that? When was he a teenage girl?

She keeps following me and Kellan around like a lost puppy. She stares at him like he's the last glass of water in the desert, and it makes my skin crawl. Why does she have to fall for Kellan? He's my best friend. He's the one thing that's only mine. We already share everything else. We shared a womb for God's sake.

The thought of the two of them kissing makes me feel sick. I'm just going to keep pretending I have no idea how they both feel, and hopefully it'll pass.

I don't miss Kayla like I thought I would, and it makes me feel weird. I thought I was in love with her, but maybe it wasn't love. She's hot and everything, and I liked spending all that time with her, but now that she's gone, I just feel free. I felt sad when she left, and I wanted to call her, I kept waiting to call her. I kept waiting, thinking she'd call me. Then the feelings started to fade. It was like in that short span of time she'd been gone, all my feelings had left, too. Is that wrong?

I set the notebook down to grab the shoes I've come for. I shouldn't be reading the notebook—it's obviously some type of journal, his secret thoughts, all the things that Danny never talked about. His feelings, his deep, personal thoughts. My fingers trace his handwriting on the pages, though—reading his journal makes me feel close to him.

It doesn't even hurt my feelings that he thought I was annoying. He's right; I've been following him and Kellan around for as long as I can remember. I never wanted to admit how much of that was because I just ached to be near them both—not just my twin brother that I loved more than anyone, but also his completely off-limits, gorgeous best friend.

The best friend who I basically banished from the house and stripped of any hope that we'd one day happen. "We" couldn't happen. Danny had hated the idea, and he never would have allowed us to have a relationship. It would have been messy, too awkward and risky for all of us. What would have happened if we had started something and then broke up? Neither of us could have avoided the other one forever with Danny in the middle.

I hate that having Kellan here was the first time I felt some peace. Even though he was torn up from the loss of Danny, too, his nearness is such a distraction from all the devastation. As much as I want to hold on to that feeling, I just can't do it. I at least owe Danny that much.

I can't let myself fall for him, anyway. I would break completely if I lost them both. So Kellan would just have to stay firmly in the friend zone. That way, we can remember Danny together, keep his memory alive.

No one knew him as we did. Sure, Dad and Uncle Dan loved him—he was their family. But they'd never love him in the same way we had, because they would never know him in all the ways that we had. His memory is our responsibility alone now.

Taking the jeans, the shoes, and his notebook with me, I head back to my room. It's time to get myself together and present Danny's last outfit to Uncle Dan and Melissa. They need to drop it off with the funeral director soon.

They're walking on eggshells around me now. They want to stress the importance of giving them the clothes, but they won't press me for fear I'll snap and go back to my bed for days on end again.

Dad's been absent from the house, so avoiding him has been simple. He's working from his office and probably doing most of the funeral prep from there, too. He's always been more comfortable making hard decisions from behind a big desk.

I am tempted almost constantly to collapse into my grief and give in to the feelings stewing just under the surface. I could easily shatter like a delicate glass ornament falling from the tallest branch on a Christmas tree. I don't, though. I refuse to let another tear leak from my eyes until this funeral is over and done. People are counting on me, and Danny deserves to be honored.

I take a deep breath. I stash the stolen journal under my pillow, sliding the jersey out from underneath and stacking it on top of his jeans and shoes. I squeeze his belongings to my chest one last time and head out of my room to relinquish them to my uncle.

15

The Night Before Chaos

It's late Thursday night, and I'm staring at the black dress I've chosen to wear to the funeral tomorrow. It's a knee-length, skater-style dress with long lace sleeves and a V-neck. I'd picked it out when we were school shopping at the beginning of the year. The beginning of the year that feels like it was months ago, not the three or so weeks the calendar says it's been.

I'd stood on the red pedestal in the middle of the little boutique shop with a wall of mirrors in front of me, like when you're shopping for a wedding dress. I'd modeled it with absolute confidence, and Danny said it made me look really grown up. When I asked him if that was a good or a bad thing, he'd rolled his eyes and said, "Just take the compliment. You look really nice."

I look at the heels I've chosen to wear with the dress and frown. If I am going to keep in the spirit of Danny, I should probably wear my red Converse instead, the matching ones we bought together in our school colors.

My stomach lurches. The ones he will be wearing when he's buried tomorrow. His body, not his soul or whatever that life force is that makes us who we are. I know that has already left his body—I saw the change with my own eyes.

I feel so alone. I want to talk to Kellan, but I already know I'll never call him. I don't know why he's the first person I think of when I need someone. I'm sure I could figure it out if I allowed myself even a few minutes to sort through all of my thoughts and feelings, but I shove them back instead. It's better this way.

I think of Sam and wonder if she's been going to school. She's called the house a few times and stopped by once before giving up. She knows me—I can be unwaveringly stubborn and withdrawn sometimes. I know I'm lucky to have her for a best friend. She's one of those best friends that people write songs about. She doesn't judge me or expect me to change.

She's probably been pacing by the phone, waiting for me to call her, to tell her I'm still breathing. But am I, really? I'm not sure what that means anymore. I know I'm still here, I think I am, but nothing resonates the same way it did before. Not talking, not eating, not even taking breaths.

As much as I want to just keep ignoring everyone, tomorrow is going to be a big day, and I don't want things to be awkward between us. I reach for my cell phone on my nightstand and reluctantly power it on.

I wait for all of the notifications to populate and then clear them out without looking at any of them. There are Facebook and Instagram alerts, voicemails, text messages. I choose to ignore them all for now. Instead, I hit the favorites button and press on Sam's name. My finger hovers over the disconnect button as the phone rings in case I lose my nerve.

"Oh my gosh, Hattie!" Sam cries into my ear on a sob when she picks up. "You made me wait so long—I've been so worried. Your Uncle Dan is the scariest ever, and he wouldn't let me in!"

"Hi," I say, chewing on my lip. "I'm sorry."

"Don't be sorry, are you... I don't know what to say. Everything sounds wrong."

"I just couldn't see anyone. I'm still not sure I'm ready," I say quietly. It's the truth, mostly. I don't think I'll tell her about Kellan's visit. It feels wrong to tell her. He was so broken, and I'm still not sure how I feel about him being the most comforting presence in my life right now.

"Don't apologize. I felt like crap bugging you like that, all the calls and everything, but I love you." She sighs heavily into the phone. "Are you going to be okay, you know, tomorrow?"

Uncle Dan said school is cancelled for Friday so any students who want to pay their respects can come. The idea that the funeral home is going to be packed with people, people that really just want in on our small town drama or an excuse to miss classes, has me feeling sick. I want people to celebrate Danny—he really deserves it. But I know there will be so many fake people, too. My hands shake thinking about having to keep it together tomorrow.

"I'm terrified..."—my voice shakes— "to see him in that box. I know it's just his body inside there, but I don't know..."

"Oh, Hattie." She cries full-on hiccupping sobs, and I gather every bit of strength I have to keep my own composure. I have to keep my promise not to break down again; I have to be strong for Danny now.

I count silently to ten.

"I'll meet you there," I say with more calm than I feel. "I'll make sure we have a seat for you up front with us. I just wanted to hear your voice for a minute." She continues to cry, and I end the call. Then I look at my bed and know I can't lay there tonight. My heart is stuck in a vice inside my chest. When I feel like this, there's only one thing my body knows to do.

I pad quietly across the bathroom floor to Danny's room, pull back the blankets on his bed, and crawl inside. His blankets smell like him. I tuck them tightly around me, wrapping myself up in a cocoon of memories and feelings, praying I've wrapped them tightly enough to hold me together. I lay there all night staring at the ceiling, knowing that goodbye is coming in a few hours, and there's nothing I can do to stop it.

16

Dress Blues

I FINALLY SEE DAD in the kitchen Friday morning. I can't avoid him on this day, and I feel a little ashamed for hiding out so long. His back is to me, and he's talking to a couple of his soldiers who have come to help with the funeral. Some of them will help carry the casket after the service—I've seen them do that in movies before but never in person. We didn't have a big service like this for Nana; it wasn't what she wanted.

He's wearing his military dress blues; all of them are. I can almost pretend we're all dressed up to go to someone's wedding since everyone looks their best. Except they don't, if you look close enough. They all have heavy eyes, dark circles, and pained expressions. It would be a horrible wedding if this was the mood of the crowd.

Dad's hair looks even more gray than usual, and I wonder how many of those gray hairs were caused by stress and grief. He's been through a lot of days like this in his lifetime but never one for his own flesh and blood, his child.

I already put on my dress and red shoes and wrangled my thick hair into a side braid. I couldn't find the energy to do anything more with it. I opted out of wearing makeup, so the circles under my eyes stick out like some kind of raccoon. It's hard for me to care what I look like on a day like today.

One of Dad's soldiers sees me around my dad's broad shoulders, and he makes what I'm sure he thinks is a sympathetic face at me. He looks more like he's in pain than anything else, and I shrug my shoulders in response. His tortured reaction is enough to stop Dad's speech mid-sentence, though; he turns to face me.

"Hattie," he breathes, looking me over from head to toe, something he's done my whole life. I always wonder what he's looking for. Gashes? Broken bones? Evidence that we actually have something in common? His eyes come back to meet mine, and he reaches an arm out, grasping my right shoulder lightly. "Are you hungry?"

His eyes. This is the moment I've avoided. Danny's eyes are staring at me, and yet, I only feel comforted. My shoulders relax.

Dad is still waiting for an answer, but eating is the last thing on my mind. I know everyone around here seems hell-bent on feeding me, but I have no hope of keeping my stomach calm today if there's food in there. I don't even have hunger pains—the pain is all centered north of my stomach region.

"No, I'm not hungry. Thanks, though," I say instead. I touch his hand that lingers on my shoulder and smile weakly at him. He's being generous, not asking me how I feel or why I've been avoiding him. Not that he would;

he's not like that. His concern is always for practical things: health and welfare, things he understands. Things he can touch and feel and fix.

He nods at me, just one quick jerk of his head, and then opens his mouth like he's going to say something more but closes it instead. He turns back to the small gathering in the kitchen, and they start discussing who is riding with whom and in what vehicles. Someone asks for directions, and I tune out of the conversation.

Danny would love this—the house is alive with people. He was always happiest in a big crowd, and I was insanely jealous of his ability to fit in with any group instantly. He lived such a loud and outgoing life. Nothing ever stopped him from going after the things he wanted—the places he could have gone if his time hadn't been cut short!

I quickly stop that train of thought—I have to keep it together. I need to stop going dark and just remember that I love him, that I am going to represent him well today.

"Dad, when do we head out?" I ask, and the room hushes again. I try not to panic when all eyes seem to be on me.

"We are leaving in a few minutes. Did you want to ride with me, or would you feel more comfortable riding with Uncle Dan and Melissa?" He doesn't give anything away with his tone or his body language. I don't know what answer he is hoping to hear from me or if he cares one way or the other.

I chew on my cheek as I think it over. I should just ride with Dad—it's what Danny would tell me to do. Suck it up, and be a part of this family no matter how unconventional we are.

"I'll ride with you." This earns me a small smile, no teeth. Not a full smile by any stretch of the imagination, but a big sign for Sergeant Major Dad. I've answered correctly, and I silently thank Danny for always pushing me in the right direction.

———————— ♡ ♡ ♡ ————————

The large, gravel parking lot at the funeral home is already filling up with cars when we arrive. The sun is shining brightly, and I'm irritated that it's such a beautiful fall day. The trees are gorgeous: Gradients of purple, red, and yellow are alive with the sounds of cicadas as the leaves shroud the old ivy-covered building with long shadows. The grass is still a saturated shade of green, holding on to the last breath of summer.

It looks like a damn Thomas Kinkade painting.

I feel like the skies should break open and pour down a torrent of punishing rain. The sky should be black, the trees barren. The world should be mourning with us. This is not a happy day.

I get out of Dad's black SUV, slamming the door unnecessarily. I'm tempted to open the door and slam it over and over again to release some of the anger vibrating through my body. I have been so emotional and filled with devastation that I was starting to get used to those feelings, but I definitely wasn't prepared for the white-hot anger that is assaulting me now. I feel sweat beading on my forehead despite the wild Texas wind. Maybe I should have forgone the thick, black tights under my dress. Too late now.

I see Sam and Kellan standing near the entrance, and I swallow back my emotions. I can't lose my shit out here in the parking lot before this thing even gets started.

Dad is talking to some people near the double front doors, and he keeps glancing my way, keeping tabs on me. Sam sees me, but she doesn't wave or move, she just watches me. They all think I'm going to lose it—I can see it in their faces. Maybe I am; what the heck do I know, anyway?

"They're opening up the viewing for just family," Uncle Dan says from beside me, and I jump. I didn't know he was there. How long has he been next to me? "Sorry if I startled you," he soothes, reaching out and taking my hand in his. "Anything you want to say before we go in?"

"Like what? That I'd rather be anywhere but here? That more than half of these people showing up aren't even here for Danny? That they're all fake and stupid, and I wish they'd just leave? That my brother shouldn't be dead, and this is all complete bullshit?!" I fist my free hand and feel the bite of my nails in my palm.

"Yes, exactly like that. Better to get it out right here with me." He pulls me into a hug, and I try to relax into his embrace. His dress blues are covered in medals and ribbons, and they press against my cheek, another reminder of the hell he and my dad have seen over the years. He's always been there for Dad but also for me and Danny. I know he really cares about my thoughts and feelings. I know he's just trying to help, but I don't feel my anger calming even after his words.

He takes my hand again and leads me to the entrance, two innocent-looking wooden doors between me and hell. Sam and Kellan look up but don't say anything. Kellan has a suit on, and his hair is gelled but still messy and flopping over on his forehead. Somehow he looks even more beautiful than usual. I wish I could pause and take the time to properly admire the view, to relax into the calm I feel around him. My heart isn't in it, though—it's time to go see my brother, ready or not.

———— ♡ ♡ ♡ ————

There are pictures everywhere inside. Long tables with red tablecloths line the entry, and each one holds at least a half dozen poster board displays. I don't know who put all the collages together, but they are works of art. I see Danny and Kellan together in almost every recent photo, but then there are hundreds of the two of us as well. Smiling, laughing, covered in mud, swimming in the lake, posing in front of the Christmas tree. I trace his face in a few of the photos, committing his smiling face full of light and life to my memory.

I'm terrified to walk through the next set of doors and see him. I'm afraid he's going to look strange, scary even, and that the corpse of my brother will be the only face I can recall afterward. I want to remember him looking like the photos on these posters. My dreams have already been haunted by the scene on the field, watching him die. That empty look I can't shake off, the moment when I knew he was gone.

The funeral home smells like an old church, like a box of musty old forgotten crayons, waxy and overwhelming, and I try not to breathe.

Uncle Dan and Dad are still talking quietly by the photos. I feel like they're stalling, always waiting on me. I hate that everyone is forced to tiptoe around my moods, but I can't seem to make it stop. So I just place one palm on each swinging door and push them softly apart.

The casket is straight ahead of me down the aisle, and pews line both sides like runway lights, guiding me. A giant cross hangs on the back wall—I forgot how much this place looks like a church. The casket is white and looks bigger than necessary, but I guess when you're over six feet tall, you need all that room. I can see the red of his jersey at the edge of my vision, but I watch my shoes as I walk.

My skin prickles with goosebumps, and my heart gallops in my chest. A burning sensation starts at the top of my head and cascades down through the soles of my feet. *Left foot, right foot,* I say in my head. *He's not here. This is just a nice ceremony, a tangible goodbye.* Having a funeral is how people find closure when their loved ones die, or so I've heard. I didn't feel closure when we saw Nana; I just felt awkward and a little scared.

When I finally reach the end, the crayon smell is replaced by the smell of fresh flowers. It's so intense it burns my nostrils. Roses, red and white, are arranged everywhere. I take a breath, place my hands on the edge of the casket, and finally lift my eyes.

Danny looks more peaceful than I was expecting. His cheeks look too rosy, his skin seems too pale, and his lips are thin and pressed into a hard line, but it does look like him. He looks like he's sleeping, dreaming even. His hair has been spiked up just how he liked it, and his hands rest on his stomach, one on top of the other. He's still beautiful, even in death. I stare at him. I have so much that I want to say, but the words won't come out.

Reaching inside, I place my hand over his. It feels cold and hard, wrong. My stomach flips, but I push through my nausea; this is the last chance I'll ever have to touch him. This is it, and I refuse to mess this up. I squeeze his fingers in my hand as I feel tears leaking from my eyes.

"Hey, jerkface." I turn my head and wipe furiously at the tears with my shoulder. "I guess this is it. I had all these poetic things to say, but now I'm here looking at your stupid beautiful face and..." I hiccup over a sob—the crushing pain is fresh all over again. Knowing I'm holding his hand in mine for the last time is making it hard to breathe. "I see your face, and I just hope you know that I love you. I love you more than anyone else in this entire world, and I always have. No one will ever come close to holding my heart the way you have, the way you always will. I'll make you proud, Danny... I promise."

I feel myself sway on my feet, so I press my knees against the stand under the casket and hope it holds me. Tears blur my vision and fall silently. I swallow the sobs back, trying hard to hold myself together. Then I lean in to kiss him softly on his forehead the way he's done to me a million times over the years. I brush my hand through his spiked hair, take one last blurry look at him, and do my best to capture this moment in my mind. Then I step back.

Dad has been waiting quietly behind me, and his eyes shine with tears. I hurry out to give him his privacy and to pull myself together.

———— ♡ ♡ ♡ ————

After getting lost and wandering around the impossibly large funeral home, I find my way to a private room reserved for the family until the service officially begins. The viewing has been opened to the public now that Dad and I have had our chance to say our goodbyes. I'm thankful that when the actual service starts, they will already have closed the casket. I don't know if I have the strength to see him that way again, though my heart does feel a little lighter somehow since I've touched him and said what I wanted to say. I hope wherever he is that he could hear me.

I thought Dad and Uncle Dan would be joining me in here, but I'm grateful for the time to myself. There's not much in this small room; it's a perfect square, probably eight feet by eight feet. Beside the ancient floral couch I'm sitting on is a small table with a lamp. Two worn-out, brown leather chairs that are cracked and peeling with age sit in the corners of the room. The crayon smell is back with a vengeance, and I try not to breathe too heavily. It at least gives me a distraction from my pain.

A knock sounds at the door, and I straighten up taller on the couch. "Come in," I say. No point in asking for a name. *Just face the music, Hattie.*

To my surprise, it's Sam. She slides through the door and shuts it back just as quick, drowning out the sounds of chatter from the hall. "Hey," she says, mascara smeared under both eyes. Her black dress makes a rustling sound as she sits next to me on the couch. Her dress is loose-fitting and sleeveless—she didn't bother with tights, and I wish I'd thought of how hot it would be inside with all of the extra bodies.

She leans in, and I let her hug me—I don't return the hug, but I lean into her a little. I'm afraid to give in, afraid I might start crying again. I'm glad I skipped the makeup today.

"How many people are here?" I pull back so I can watch her face to see if she's telling me the truth. Sam doesn't lie well—her eyes go all shifty.

"Too many," she says and then finally meets my gaze. "I think the entire school is here."

I try not to be upset by the news. I knew this was how it would be, one of the downsides of living in a small town. Especially since we've been here for so many years now. The entire town knows Danny from football, knows number twelve is Danny Tate—or was. The quarterback that will take our team all the way... or who would have, anyway.

"I think Kellan was looking for you a little while ago," Sam says timidly. "Have you talked to him?"

My mind flashes to him on the floor in Danny's room, and I grip the edge of the couch. It's so hard to keep my mind from wandering to him, wondering how he's dealing with all of this. He loved Danny even more than most. I want to find comfort in his arms, to talk to him about Danny until I can't talk anymore. The guilt is still there, though; I taste it on my tongue. I can't get that close to him again—it's not an option.

"No. I'll find him after maybe." I try not to give anything away. I decide that it's better not to talk about him at all—my heart might betray me.

Smoothing my hands over my lap, I listen to the echoing commotion beyond the door. A quick glance at my watch says it's just about time to head into the ceremony.

I'd left my phone at home in my bedroom. After talking to Sam last night, I switched it to silent mode and threw it in my nightstand. I didn't want to talk to anyone else right now—well, anyone I was allowing myself to talk to anyway.

"Shall we head in now?" Sam swallows nervously. "I told your dad I'd sing a song before the service kicks off. But, I mean, I'll wait with you until you're ready, of course…"

"I'm ready," I say, feeling anything but ready for this.

Sam stands up before everyone. She's wearing black ballet flats, and her hair is pulled into a pretty braided crown, her signature performance hair. She looks angelic as usual, and I'm captivated by her before she even sings the first note.

She takes a deep breath, someone starts the music, and then she begins singing. Her voice is fluid and graceful, and the sad lyrics are haunting. She's chosen to sing "Be Still" by The Fray. Danny would have loved it. They're his favorite band, and the words cut right through me. He's with me—whether I can feel it or not, my brother has to be here with me.

There isn't a dry eye in the house when she finishes, and she comes to sit in her spot beside me. I take her hand in mine and hold on tight.

The service is going beautifully, and after the pastor says a few nice things about Danny, some of his teammates come up to tell stories about him. Most of them are hilarious; typical Danny, the life of the party. Some are really sweet stories. Sarah, the girl he just gushed about to Kellan a few days ago, comes up to tell a story. She talks about how Danny was always the first to offer help if someone needed something. He'd changed a flat tire for her one night over the summer, and then he didn't tell anyone about it or expect any kind of thank you or payment. He was one of the good ones, she says.

The house is packed—even the standing room is crammed with people. Some people are even outside the open doors, peering in between the crowd. I breathe through the annoyance. If they want to be here, then fine. At least Danny is probably getting a kick out of the scene—he lived for attention like this.

I am sandwiched between Dad and Sam. On Sam's other side, Kellan is sitting with his parents. Uncle Dan and Melissa and Coach and his wife are further down but still on our pew. We are a strange-looking group, decked out in military dress uniforms and clothes that match the rings around our eyes: black, the color of despair.

Kellan stands and climbs the four steps to the podium. I watch him and notice his normal long, confident stride seems tense and small. His hands shake as he adjusts the microphone for his height. His dark-brown eyes shine black as he looks at me and then back at the crowd before him.

"I've never been the religious type; I don't know exactly what I believe about life and death and creation and all those things. What I do believe in is brotherhood. Danny and I had that; true brotherhood. I have four older brothers, but none of them felt as real to me as Danny did. We had the kind of friendship that you didn't have to question; if he needed me, I would be there. If I ever needed him, he seemed to know that without even having to ask.

"The memories I have of him are many, and I will never let those fade. I feel a responsibility now to keep his memory alive for the rest of my life. Since I'm not a man of faith per se, I'm not sure exactly what happens to us when we die. I don't know where we go or what becomes of the essence of someone. What I do know, what I'm absolutely certain of, is that some really amazing people have gone before us. As long as we go where they did, we will be in good company." He looks down at the casket then, drumming the top with his fingertips. Tears shimmer in his eyes. "Rest easy, brother; I'll take it from here."

He nods at the crowd, tears slipping down his cheeks, and then walks back to his seat in the pew. I keep my eyes focused on the podium, his words warming me to the core.

He loved my brother so much, and that was a gift in itself, but that speech was vulnerable and heartfelt. He is getting to me all over again.

"Would you like to say something?" Dad asks softly, resting his hand on my knee with a soft squeeze. "You don't have to, but I want you to know that you can."

I don't even know what I'd say up there. I already said what I wanted to when I saw Danny's body earlier, and Kellan had said everything else. I shake my head. "I can't."

Dad nods at me and pats my shoulder. We all watch him step up to the podium to deliver the eulogy.

"Anyone who ever met Danny fell in love with him instantly. He had that fun-loving spirit that we all envy and a pretty face that got him out of more than his fair share of trouble. He had the biggest heart, and he would gladly give you the shirt off his back. He wasn't fond of goodbyes, spiders, or taking things too seriously.

"He was brilliant minded, but he always tried to hide how smart he was. He liked being the fun guy—he didn't want to be known as the brain. He always said Hattie was the brains of the family, and no one needed two brains. Danny and Hattie had the kind of sibling bond that you read about in fairy tales. It went deeper than just a twin bond. Watching them grow up together, watching them care for each other, was the most amazing thing. I was the lucky one to have him for a son. I'm not sure I've ever known a better man." Dad's voice wavers a little, and he looks at me again before continuing.

I try to stay focused on my dad's words, but my mind floats away from me. Maybe it's self-preservation, but the next thing I know, he's finishing up, and I can't account for how much time has passed.

"If anyone else would like to say something, please come up now. Otherwise, thank you for coming to celebrate my boy. It means the world to us that you all came out to help us honor him." Dad is searching the crowd with his eyes, and his words are hitting my soul.

I'm barely holding it together. I never knew Dad thought any of that. He never shares personal things like that. Tears burn in my throat.

From the back of the room, the crowd begins to part—someone is coming up from the back to say something. Whoever it is they are short, and I can't see them through the throngs of people who are moving out of the way as much as they can.

But I know something is wrong, because when I look back at Dad, his mouth is pressed in a hard, thin line, and his face is devoid of color. It takes a lot to rattle Dad.

—— ♡ ♡ ♡ ——

The woman is short, probably close to my height, but I can't see her face—her back is to me when she climbs the steps to the podium. She's wearing a red dress, and it looks so wrong in a sea of blue and black funeral clothes. Dad is still stunned into silence, just staring at her. Her hair is swept up into an elaborate, dark-brown twist on the back of her head. She's thin and petite and walks with purpose.

She finally turns to face the room, and I freeze.

I don't immediately recognize her face, but it is too similar to my own to ignore the obvious. Swap out my round, green eyes for her smaller blue ones, widen her nose just a tad, and we are the same.

I know without a doubt that this woman is my mother. I haven't seen a picture of her since I was a small child, but I know it's her with certainty. Shock quickly fades, and bitterness takes its place. Red-hot tongues of anger lick up my legs and burst across my chest, and soon I am an inferno of fury. How dare she show her face today, and here of all places!

Propelled by the white heat in my veins, my feet move on their own, like someone else has taken over my body. She's speaking into the microphone, but I cannot hear the words she's saying over the roaring in my ears. I can hardly see her through the haze of anger clouding my eyes—she's just a blob of red in front of me.

"What the hell are you doing here," I growl from deep within my throat, and it's not a question. I shove her away from the podium, and she gasps at me. Her eyes go wide.

"Henrietta," she breathes and reaches out as if she plans to embrace me.

"Don't you *dare* touch me!" I scream. People are whispering loudly to each other, and I'm sure all eyes are glued to the scene I'm making, but I couldn't care if I tried. "You're not welcome here! No one wants you here! Why don't you do what you do best and LEAVE!" Someone's hands are grabbing at me, but I'm too wild, too wound up with grief and anger and so many emotions I can't even name. Adrenaline propels me forward, and I throw fists and elbows at the arms that try to subdue me. "GET OUT!

JUST GET OUT! HE'S DEAD; WHAT GOOD ARE YOU TO US NOW?"

Her face turns cold, and her eyes are ice. She doesn't cry or shout back at me—she just shakes her head and turns to Dad. "You promised me you'd take care of them," she snarls.

I see pain flash in his eyes, and his torment is the final straw. How dare she say that to Dad? He didn't leave us; he didn't abandon his children. She did.

I wind back and let my fist fly into her face.

17

What a Hothead

I'M NOT A VIOLENT person by nature; I would much rather avoid conflict at all costs. I've always been the peacekeeper. But at some point, wanting to keep the peace meant turning into a doormat, and I am done letting people stomp on me.

It's not like I haven't learned how to fight. After all, I grew up surrounded by men. Not just any men, either: a brother who wasn't about to let me off easy and a revolving door of tough-as-nails soldiers with something to prove. So I learned how to fight or, more accurately, how to defend myself, from a young age. Most girls probably wouldn't have suffered a knee-jerk reaction and punched their mother in the face. But I'm not most girls—this has been the worst week of my life, and she's not exactly the picture of a loving mother.

As soon as my fist made contact, I felt, more than heard, the sickening crack. I imagine I broke her nose, but I don't get a chance to see what kind of damage I've done. Somehow Kellan manages to grab me from behind and pull me down off the stage. I have unleashed utter chaos, and the cacophony of hushed voices assaults the formerly silent room. I try to find my dad's face in the commotion, but Kellan is dragging my body through the crowd and out the emergency exit.

When the hot air hits my face, I exhale hard. I lean over and tuck my head into my chest, sucking in air. The adrenaline in my veins slows, my face is hot, and I still feel the anger, but now I also feel shame sneaking in.

"You okay?" Kellan is rubbing his hand in circles on my back. I stare at his shiny black shoes that are sinking into the thick, green lawn.

"I can't believe I did that..." My breathing is ragged. I still can't quite catch my breath.

"You definitely landed that punch," he says.

I straighten up to meet his eyes. "Good. She deserved it."

"Is that the first time you've seen her since she left?" he asks, his hand frozen on my back. I'd almost forgotten that Kellan knows everything about my mother. Well, everything that Danny and I knew, at least.

"Yes, and I definitely never imagined it going like this." I try to smile, but it feels wrong. Emotions churn in my body, a whirlpool of them threatening to suck me into oblivion. No one has followed us out, so I hope the situation inside is under control. Dad is going to kill me, and I probably deserve it.

"Did you imagine it?" Kellan oozes calm, but he looks at me curiously. His quiet demeanor is helping me slow my breathing and settle my nerves. I squat down and sit in the grass. We're directly under the shade of giant trees here, and the only sound I hear is coming from the cicadas overhead. I sit and stare out into the cemetery, and he joins me, taking my hand in his. I let him, happy for the distraction of physical contact.

"I've been thinking about her a lot lately, even though I try not to. Danny and I just talked about her the other day, actually. Debating if we'd want to talk to her should we have the chance." I can still hear his voice from that morning in his car when he said he would want to ask her why she left Dad. He wanted to know how she could walk out on us and not look back. Did she even cry for us? "I didn't think I cared one way or the other if I ever got to ask her anything. Danny did, though—he wanted answers. Ironic, huh?"

Kellan nods, tracing figure-eight patterns on my palm. "Do you think you want to ask her questions now? Hear her side of the story?" His expression is blank, but I feel like there's probably a right and a wrong way to answer this question. I'm not really sure which is which, though.

So I close my eyes and picture Danny sitting here with us. I try to imagine what he would say about all of this. He'd tell me the right way to handle this mess. He was always better at defusing a situation, seeing it from all sides.

"I mean, I just smashed her face. I doubt she wants to talk to me." I sidestep the question. I don't know if I'm ready to answer the tough questions right now. I'm not in my right mind, clearly. It's been a day already, and we haven't even finished burying my brother.

I wish I could just rewind time, go back to Thursday before my whole world imploded and just sit in my boring health class, enjoying the blissful ignorance of how brutal life can really be.

"I was pretty shocked when you let that fist fly." Kellan chuckles, lacing his fingers with mine. "I doubt anyone is going to blame you, though. It's a small town, Hattie—people know what she did. They also know you've been through a lot this week. I bet she'll forgive you."

I yank my hand out of his; I feel like he's punched me in the stomach. "Forgive me?" I ask. My cheeks had begun to cool from the fresh air, but now a second wave of heat rises up my face. "Why would I need her forgiveness? If anything, she should be begging for mine!"

"Hattie, don't you think that's kind of harsh?" His eyes narrow at me.

I push off the ground and wipe my hands on my dress. I can't believe he's taking her side! I stomp toward the parking lot and hope like hell that Dad left the car unlocked. So much for Kellan being a calming influence.

"Hattie, wait! Don't you think you should hear her side before you just shut her out? She's your mom!"

I spin on him then, anger rising to the surface again. It doesn't ever seem far from me lately—it lives in my skin, in my bones.

"Mom? She's not my mom. You have a mom, someone who loves you and puts you first. You don't know the first thing about someone you love abandoning you by choice! So just leave me alone! You like her so much, *you* go talk to her!"

"You know what? I think you're being really selfish! You're not the only one who lost Danny. We all did—we're all hurting. You don't get to have a monopoly on grief!" Tears slide down Kellan's face, and his jaw looks rigid enough to crack.

"A monopoly on grief?" I laugh, but it's not funny. "If that's how you *really* feel about me, then leave me the hell alone!" I yank hard on the driver side door of Dad's SUV, and it swings open. I climb in and slam the door behind me, locking Kellan out before he can stop me. Not that he tries. When I look out the window, he's already stalking back toward the funeral home and doesn't even glance back my way. *Good, take that crap somewhere else.*

This day has gone even worse than I ever could have imagined. I don't want to be here anymore, and they haven't even brought Danny out to the cemetery yet.

If anyone really wants to come and find me, they will, so I recline the chair as far as it will go and lie back. I try to calm myself down the way Danny taught me when we were small. *Visualize something that makes you feel safe, calm.* That's what he'd say now. I close my eyes and picture Danny laughing, eating popcorn in bed while we watch *Teen Wolf*, yelling at me over leaving my dirty towels in the bathroom. I see him so perfectly, so vividly, and I hope like hell I can always remember him this way.

———— ♡ ♡ ♡ ————

When they finally carry the casket out to the cemetery, I watch the procession through the car window. Four of Dad's men are on either side—dress blues, white gloves—with Dad and Kellan at the front. Danny wasn't a soldier, so he didn't warrant a military funeral, but these soldiers are doing everything they can to honor him as one of their own. It's too hot to stay hidden in the car—sweat is trickling down the back of my dress—so once I am positive everyone is out of the building and distracted, I slip out of the car and make my way through the crowd to the burial site.

The sea of blues and blacks are hunched, swaying to imaginary melancholy music. The wind rustles through the leaves above, but it feels eerily quiet for such a large group. Even the cicadas seem to have lost their voices.

And I see so many stoic and tear-streaked faces. I had expected these people to be snickering, laughing, doing all the inappropriate things teenagers do. Instead, everyone is being respectful. Maybe everyone here really is mourning the loss of my brother. I may have been quick to judge and wasted my energy being mad at the wrong people.

The pastor is saying his final blessing as they lower the casket into the ground. I watch in silence, blending in with the crowd but shivering against the depth of my loneliness. Kellan, Sam, even Dad... none of them seem to understand how I am feeling. They loved him, too, and they lost him just like I did, but my entire world feels changed forever.

I'm not trying to say my pain is worse, but I just can't see around it. I'm encompassed by darkness. I'm begging someone to recognize that I am drowning. I've lost the other half of my soul.

I try to remember all the things people say when someone dies, something comforting. I know that when

Nana died, someone told me to close my eyes, and I'd feel her with me. I tried to for weeks, but I didn't feel anything.

Maybe you have to be really close to God to feel it. I used to feel secure in my faith. I used to believe you could pray for things, and people would get better or come home. I used to believe in miracles, in magic, in things just working out.

For me, though, prayers seem to go unanswered. Maybe I am being punished for not believing hard enough. I prayed on the field that night, prayed they'd save him, prayed that he'd make it through somehow. I begged God to let him be alright, and still, he died.

Watching from a distance, I see Dad toss the first handful of dirt, and I try not to flinch. I close my eyes and will myself to feel Danny with me, to know that he is out there somewhere: his spirit, his energy, his essence, whatever we amount to when our bodies no longer serve us. Not down in that box, in the dark, alone.

Why can't I feel you?

I take one last look at my friends and family saying their final goodbyes, and I'm relieved that my mother is not present. Then I turn on my heel and head for the road. Walking home might be just what the doctor ordered.

———— ♡ ♡ ♡ ————

I am almost halfway home when Dad's car pulls up beside me. His window creaks in protest as it lowers, and he regards me with weary eyes. "Would you like to get in? Or do you need to walk it off?"

I appreciate, maybe for the first time in my life, that Dad used the word "need" instead of "want." Like he understands my need to move, to reflect quietly on my own.

"I'll just meet you at home," I say, giving him a slight wave.

"We *will* talk later." It's not up for debate—I hear it in his voice. He rolls up his window and drives on, down the winding, tree-lined street ahead of me. Everything looks so beautiful, but my mood refuses to lighten.

My mind races with questions.

Do I want to meet my mother? To ask her questions? To understand her side of the story like Kellan had suggested? I am still angry that he's taken her side. I thought he cared about me! I thought we were friends! How dare he call me selfish!

I shake my head. I'm overheated, but I wish I had pockets to jam my hands in. Even though the wind is blowing hard, there is too much humidity in the air, and my skin is slick with sweat. I should have asked Dad for a water bottle from his car.

At least the heat will help keep me focused and moving.

Maybe I could talk to Dad about everything. He'd had to deal with the aftermath of my violent and disruptive outburst at the funeral, after all. Maybe he had an idea of what Mom was going to say or could tell me what she said after I attacked her.

I'm sure the kids at school will be talking about that for a while. Crazy Hattie, finally lost her marbles. Everyone always fears the introverts, and maybe they should. We're like ticking time bombs hiding in plain sight.

But whether people are talking about me or not, I need to go back to school. Anything to keep me from crawling back into Danny's bed and never getting out.

18

Debriefing Dad

I'VE NEVER SEEN MY father truly let go and cry. The tears in his eyes at the funeral are the first I've ever seen for myself. He's all hard lines and ridges, rules and authority. He's order personified. According to Nana, he didn't even cry when our mother left him. Uncle Dan says he cried when their best friend died overseas, but I just couldn't visualize it. I'd always doubted the validity of that story.

He sits down next to me on my bed, and the mattress sinks to accommodate his heavy frame. When I walked in the door earlier, he told me to take a shower, that he'd be in to talk to me in awhile. Now that he's here, I'm anticipating some consequences for my unforgivable behavior today. For once, I really can't blame him for being so angry with me.

The first time I've ever seen cracks in his hard exterior was when he saw Mom at the funeral, but I've never seen him nervous like this. His lips are pulled into a tight, thin line, and his eyes, that are normally identical in hue to my own, look tired and flat. His skin is papery white, like when you're sick and trying not to vomit. He's almost unrecognizable, as if someone sucked all the color out of his body and left him ashen.

He's fidgeting with the ridiculous frills on my bedspread and hasn't made eye contact with me. But this is Sergeant Dad—he doesn't fidget. He's always staring me down with those all-seeing eyes, the signature of this family. Dad, Danny, and me.

Oh, Danny. My heart spasms in my chest.

We don't do deep conversations—we barely converse at all. But I'm not sure what to expect from this stranger in my dad's body. I'm sure he's furious with me; maybe that's the reason for his strange behavior. Maybe I'm finally being sent to military school. Public hysteria is his biggest pet peeve, and I have been beyond hysterical. I was violent even, not the shy girl everyone knows me to be. He likes to be in constant control, a definite side effect of his years in the military. No nonsense. And I have obliterated all of his rules.

"Henrietta..." he breathes.

My full name—this can't be good. I feel myself shrink a little, pulling at my oversized t-shirt. The last thing I want to do is cause this family more heartache, yet I've embarrassed us on a day that wasn't even supposed to be about me. A little piece of me knows Danny would have enjoyed the show, though—he'd be proud that I stood up for Dad.

"Henrietta, I'm sorry." His voice is too high and cracks on the last word, and I'm instantly alert. I watch him closely, taking him all in. His scarred hands, his shoulders rigid with tension... and there's something else. He seems...

afraid. He's apologizing to me when I know I'm the one that owes the apologies.

"I've seen unthinkable things in my lifetime. Buried so many good men." He takes a breath. "I was blindsided when your mother left, and I know I didn't handle that as well as I could have. I left you two to fend for yourselves. I won't make excuses for that, but I am sorry."

My heart hammers in my chest, threatening to burst through my ribcage altogether. Could your own heart bruise your ribs? That's what it feels like. I don't know how to process these new emotions, so I just nod my head for him to continue. I don't trust my own voice.

"None of what I've experienced in my fifty years has prepared me for losing Danny. Not war, not losing my best friend, not your mother..." He pauses, tears making tracks down his flushed, papery skin.

"Hattie, no one was as close to Danny as you, and I'm afraid. I'm afraid that this loss is too big for you, for me. I'm afraid I'll lose you, too. I know you don't need me, neither of you ever have"—he swallows audibly—"but I hope that you'll let me in. That you'll talk to me. Let me shoulder this burden; let me carry some of this pain. Let someone in, anyone. Whatever it takes, Hattie; just don't disappear on me. I cannot bury another child."

I watch him run his hands through his silver hair, tears splattering the comforter like polka dots. I no longer have Danny, my rock, the only family I've ever felt close to, and I don't know this man sitting next to me. I don't know him, but, oh God, I want to.

Dad will have to do a lot more talking for me to trust him with the important stuff, but he is trying, right? Is this some kind of olive branch? I know this must have cost him, pushing through his own walls and fears to open up to me. He could have abandoned us, too, just like Mom had, but he is still here, still fighting. Still trying to figure everything out, just like the rest of us.

He hasn't said a word about me punching her. He hasn't said a word about my horrible behavior, either; he's just pouring his heart out to me, and it's catching me completely off guard. The walls around me are crashing down like they've been hit with explosives. A complete demolition crew just rode in on those tears on his face, and all my reservations were destroyed.

I hesitate for a moment, but then my heart wins the battle over my reservations, and I launch myself into his arms. Sobs wrack my body as I cling to his strong shoulders and let myself cry. He's stiff at first, but then his arms come around me and hold firm, holding the pieces of me together. Our bodies meld with grief and understanding, and he lets out a breath as his big frame shakes. He is warm and solid, my safety and comfort. He's the anchor I didn't realize I was looking for. He smells like cedar soap and cinnamon, and I breathe him in, afraid this is all a dream, and I'll soon wake up.

"You're wrong, Dad," I finally croak out. "We always needed you."

He kisses the top of my head. I snuggle deeper into his lap like I remember doing as a small child, and, for the first time in days, I allow myself to give in to sleep.

19

Two Steps Forward

I WAKE UP LATE on Saturday morning—I've finally slept through the night. I don't remember Dad leaving my room, but he's gone now, so I hug my comforter to my chest and try to stay in the haze of sleep a little longer. That conversation with Dad was probably the deepest one in Tate family history, but I still need to talk to him about Mom. I don't know how he's going to take it.

He never mentioned her at all, and that was odd. Maybe he was avoiding it like I wished I could. I could talk to Uncle Dan, but something tells me going directly to the source is the better call. I stretch my arms over my head, yawning and squirming in my bed. It is time to get up, get ready, and face my fears.

I smell bacon in the hallway, and my stomach growls. I haven't eaten anything substantial for days. My lack of food is starting to take its toll, and I take hunger pains as a good sign.

I turn the corner at the end of the hall and stop in my tracks. Dad is cooking bacon at the stove, and Uncle Dan is chopping veggies near the sink. Melissa is reading a book while sipping coffee from her perch on one of the barstools. I almost laugh seeing the two men cooking while Melissa kicks back and enjoys her reading. I smile at her. She knows how to hold her own with the men, and I admire that.

I sit on a barstool next to her, and everyone stops what they are doing to look at me. "That bacon smells amazing, Dad. I hope there's enough for me." That earns me not one, but three wide smiles. This is the first time since Danny that I have asked for food outright.

I still want to have that important conversation with Dad, but it can wait until we've all eaten breakfast.

After we eat, I ask Dad if we can talk. He tells me he has to make a quick call, and then he'll meet me in his office.

I love Dad's office, so I slip inside to wait for him. A wall of bookshelves sits behind a dark mahogany desk and chocolate leather desk chair. Floor-to-ceiling bookshelves are packed with everything from business strategies to Beowulf. I definitely inherited my love of reading from Dad. His office isn't huge, but it is elegant and handsome, from the small gold chandelier that casts a warm glow over the space to the wood and leather accents. Even the walls are painted a rich, green color that just screams old library charm. The smell of books fills the air, and the scent has a calming effect on my nerves.

Belle would feel at home here, and Dad isn't quite as bad as the Beast.

I flop down in one of the leather chairs across from Dad's desk and wait. I'm still trying to think of the right way to bring up my thoughts on the Mom situation.

I don't wait long before he comes in to meet me, but as soon as I see his face, I brace for impact.

"I want to hear what you have to say," he says somberly, "and then I have some news of my own." His knees give, and he drops heavily into his chair, resting his arms on the desk. He looks so tired, and I feel partially to blame for his exhaustion. I briefly wonder if the conversation I want to have is asking too much of him, but I shake it off and force my mouth to move.

"I want to talk about Mom." I spit the words out. I watch his face for surprise or panic but see neither, which lifts my confidence. "I want to know if you've talked to her since she's been here and if she had anything worthwhile to say." I cross my legs underneath me and chew on my lip while I wait for his response.

Steepling his fingers, Dad takes a loud breath. "I talked to her after the funeral briefly. I was not thrilled with the way she blindsided all of us at the service; she could have simply let us know that she intended to come..." He pauses. "She said she didn't know she was coming until she found herself in her car driving here. She's always been impulsive like that. She doesn't take the time to consider anyone else's feelings—that's just not how she operates."

"Why did she leave, Dad? Do you know?" I know this is probably painful for him, rehashing old feelings, but I can't stop the questions from coming now that I have allowed myself to ask them.

"She said motherhood was too much for her. That she thought that's what she wanted, but then once you and Danny came, she didn't want it anymore. As if we were talking about curtains she wanted to return to the store."

He throws his hands up in the air. "You two were easy babies—wonderful, really. Everyone complimented us on how easy you were to care for despite being twins. Neither of you was a complainer or sickly or any of the things new parents are warned about. When I was deployed, I understood that she might've felt overwhelmed, so I offered to pay for a nanny so she could get out, do whatever she wanted for a few hours a day. She had plenty of friends in the military community. She didn't have her family near, but she'd never had that. I thought it was just new-mom jitters, and she'd get past it all."

"But she didn't... get past it?" I ask him, but I already know the answer. If she had gotten past it, she wouldn't have left us.

"No, she got worse. The older you two got, the less attention you needed from her, and I thought it was helping. Then one night, in the middle of the night, she went to the grocery store. She just left the two of you there in your room. Luckily, neither of you noticed, and you both slept through the whole ordeal. But it was one of the scariest moments of my life."

Dad looks a million miles away as he continues.

"I'd asked the neighbor lady to look after your mother while I was on twenty-four-hour duty that night. I just had a bad feeling about the whole thing, leaving her alone for that long. I guess the neighbor saw her leave without you and panicked, tried to get inside but couldn't because the doors were locked."

I bite the inside of my cheek to keep from commenting. I don't want to discourage him.

"I called the police and rushed home as fast as I could. When she got home, the police were there taking a statement from me. The thing is, I wasn't sure what I'd find inside. I wasn't sure if she'd hurt you or left you where you could hurt yourselves. You were almost six then, but kids can still get hurt so easily. I was terrified and horrified at the same time. I couldn't imagine leaving her alone with you for another deployment knowing how careless she'd been.

"She was furious and wanted to know what I was doing there. Why I was questioning her parenting choices so much, why I would involve the police in our personal life." He shakes his head like he's clearing the memory from his vision. His hands are white against the wooden desk. "I wanted to ask her to leave, to go get some help or take a vacation or whatever it was she needed to do to get her head on straight. Get her emotions squared away or whatever the issue was. Soldiers go through big changes after going to war, so I thought maybe she could talk to someone, and then she'd be okay." He takes a deep breath and runs a hand through his hair like Danny used to do. I have never noticed how many mannerisms they share before. Now it is all I can see.

I don't rush him; I just sit quietly and wait for him to continue.

"I never got the chance. She went straight to our room, grabbed an army duffle, started throwing all her clothes inside, and took off her ring, throwing it at my head. She told me I could go to hell, that if I was such a good parent, I could take care of the two of you all by myself. She said she was getting out of that place for good.

"I wasn't good at talking about my feelings. I still struggle with it"—he gestures between us and gives me a half-smile—"but I'm trying."

"You're doing fine, Dad." My voice sounds quiet. I know I should feel some outrage or shock, but mostly I just feel sad for Dad. I can see how much these memories still hurt, how much he really lost that day.

"I probably could have begged her to stay or insisted that she go get help. I was so afraid she'd hurt you or just disappear into the night and leave you alone... so I just let her go. I called your nana the next day, and she moved in with us by the weekend. I tried to find your mom a few times that first year, but when I heard nothing from her, I just assumed she was better off wherever she'd gone and that we would be better off without her. It broke me listening to Danny cry for her night after night."

He puts his head in his hands, elbows digging into the desktop from the force. "I don't know if I ever made a single right decision for you kids."

I unfold my legs and stand. Tears are streaming down my face, but they're not for my mother—they are for my dad. Listening to him explain his pain and his experience with Mom has shifted my own view of the past. Dad did everything he could to protect us, to love us, to keep us safe and happy. I only saw the overprotective side, the annoyingly anal Sergeant Dad. I never knew it went so much deeper than wanting a clean house and absolute control.

I wish he would have told me all of this before, when Danny was still here and could see this part of Dad, too. Danny always saw Dad better than I did. I don't know how many times he told me to try to see things from Dad's side, and I just waved him off.

I walk around the desk and hug him from behind. This is the second time in less than twenty-four hours that we have bonded over the truth. Dad is letting some of his feelings out, and we have shared the physical contact I have craved from him.

He slips his arm around my back and holds me close, a small sob escaping from him. "I love you kids more than anything, and I should have told you both more."

I nod against him. "Is she still in town?"

I know it was the wrong thing to ask when he stiffens. "You want to see her?" He looks up into my eyes wearily.

I want to say no, that the woman can go back to whatever hole she's been hiding in for the last eleven years, but at some point, my stance shifted. I want her to have to tell me to my face that she doesn't love me enough to stay. I want to close the book on this chapter and then burn it. "I just want closure."

"She's staying at the Fremont Hotel if you really want to see her. I'll go with you if you want me to; I just don't want her to hurt you. She's not the woman that I thought she was all those years ago." He hugs me a little tighter and kisses my head again. I can get used to this.

"I don't mind going alone; I don't have that much to say to her." I don't want him to go through that, and I really can hold my own. Then I remember he had something he wanted to tell me. "You had news?" I ask.

Dad sighs, pulling out of our embrace to face me head-on. "I know this is the worst possible timing, but I have some business that can't wait overseas. My guys depend on me, and I need to take care of some emergent issues that have come up. Uncle Dan and Melissa have offered to stay here with you while I'm gone. I'm hoping it won't take more than two weeks."

I feel like he's slapped me. All this work we've been doing, and he's going to leave me again, just like that. I try not to pout, but I feel like a small child who has just been told that Christmas is canceled because Santa isn't real. *Grow up, Hattie.*

"Can't someone else do it?" I ask. I know I'm being selfish, but I don't care. I don't want to be alone. Danny isn't here, and that fact will be even more obvious with Dad gone. Uncle Dan is great, but it feels weird having him and Melissa around right now. I just want things to feel as normal as they can. No more changes; I'm trying to catch my breath here!

"I wish I could send someone else. I am working on something to keep this sort of thing from happening; I've spent too much time away from you already. I'm ready to let someone else take the reins a little." He scrubs a hand over his stubble. "I'm sorry, Hattie, but I just can't get out of this one. It's my company and my responsibility."

I take a few small steps back from his chair, each step putting more than just physical distance between us. His eyes watch my retreat, and I see rejection flash across them. "Whatever. When are you leaving?" He can't hurt me if I don't let him get any closer than I already have this weekend. His company is somehow a more important responsibility than being here for his daughter?

I know better than to trust things will keep going how I want. Everyone I love leaves me behind. Even Danny.

"Hattie…" He reaches for me, but I remain where I am, just out of his grasp, the place he's always been to me. I am waiting for him to finish talking so I can escape this room and these warring emotions inside me.

His hand falls when he realizes I'm not going to budge, and he flinches. "I need to leave in the next hour. It's a long flight, and I need to get out as soon as possible."

Immediate. Not days, not even hours. No time to wrap my mind around the idea. No time at all before he flies halfway around the world to who even knows where to risk his life for his country. It doesn't matter that he's not in the military anymore; being a contractor is just as dangerous and apparently just as demanding of his time.

Plus, the terrorists don't care who their rockets or bullets hit—any American will do. Dad has been in more close calls than he will admit. I figured this out after comparing stories between him and Uncle Dan. Sometimes Uncle Dan forgets that Dad doesn't tell us very much, so he's a goldmine of private and forbidden information.

My heart aches. I'm torn between wanting to run into his arms and wanting to beat my fists on his chest or the floor and beg him not to leave me again. Why do I feel this way so often these days? I feel like my body is pulling apart into two halves, and the split is killing me. I'm so torn between pushing people away and holding them as close as I can in case it's the last time I get the chance. My entire world is turned upside down, and I don't know the rules anymore. Nothing makes any sense. My head is spinning, and my heart is breaking, and all I can say is "okay."

I turn away from him so he won't see the tears in my eyes and swallow over the lump building in my throat. I walk slowly and controlled until I'm sure he can't see me, and then I run to Danny's room and shut myself in his closet. I curl up on the floor and inhale his scent, letting it wash over me. I will spend the next few hours building the walls back up around my heart. I just hope that it's enough to save me from complete and utter annihilation.

I fall asleep in Danny's closet and wake up stiff and cold from lying on the floor. I sit up and try to orient myself, seeing the stacks of Danny's journals near my feet. I remember the one I have tucked under my pillow. I want to read more of his words, but not today, not when my heart is reeling knowing Dad is already gone.

I tell myself that things are going to be fine. That I am going to find a new normal and get through this. Maybe if I say it enough times, I'll start to believe it. I doubt it.

I have to get back to school. I am surely falling behind. I know my teachers will work with me; they have been sending home assignments and lesson plans and allowing me to do as much from home as they can, but I haven't put any effort into my schoolwork. There are so many participation grades and group projects that you have to be present for, and even with leniency, my AP classes are easy to fail. I didn't change that much overnight. I am still the crazy-dedicated student I have always been under this hard-shell coating of grief. I still want to get into a school on scholarships and get out of McKinley Lake... don't I?

Do I?

What does the future look like now that Danny won't be in it? I have always planned to leave home and go to school—I just thought we would do it together. That Danny would help me get through the painful social part of it all. Forever my security blanket, my biggest protector.

For some reason, picturing any kind of future without him doesn't seem possible.

But I will go back. I will go back to school, and I will work even harder. I'll put all my focus on school and learning and let everything else go to the back of my mind.

This could be the distraction I need: to get back into my own routine. To feel like me again. Because I don't know who this girl is, this stranger in my body that has become an only child. I don't know what she wants or how she's going to navigate all these big feelings alone.

Alone.

Everything without Danny just feels lonely. I know that's not fair. I know there are people around me that care about me and love me. I just also know that when you care about people and trust them, they have a tendency to leave.

My mind immediately goes to Sam and Kellan. They've gone out of their way to let me have my space, to let me get through all these emotions, and I've been pretty intolerable and ungrateful. I practically took Kellan's head off for disagreeing with me about talking to my mom, and now that's exactly what I plan to do.

And Sam. We have practically talked every day since we met, and now I've made her wait days for a response. If I want to have any friends left when the dust settles, I need to get myself together. I can be mature and deal with this, can't I? I don't have to feel better to be nicer to everyone. This whole grieving thing is like a huge battering ram. It's crashing into everything in my life, and I don't want any more casualties.

I pick myself up off the floor and head to the shower, a plan forming in my head. I will make myself presentable for the public and get out of the house. I'll go see Sam and then make a plan to get back to school on Monday. My life might be in shambles, but it has to go on. I just hope that keeping busy will distract me from the crushing weight on my heart.

———— ♡ ♡ ♡ ————

It's hot and sticky outside, so I opt for comfort over style. I throw on my favorite pair of jean shorts, a plain, white, v-neck shirt, and the first pair of sandals I can find, the black sparkle pair I borrowed from Sam when we went to the lake. "I'm heading out," I yell to whoever is listening, beelining for the front door.

"Whoa! It's pretty hot out there—you want a ride somewhere, Tate?" one of Dad's remaining soldiers asks me. He is tall and skinny and very young—he can't be older than mid-twenties. He has jeans and a "Go Army" t-shirt on, and his hair is buzzed almost to the skin.

No one has called me Tate for a long time. Danny was Tate, on and off the field, but not me.

I hesitate. It *would* be nice to not have to walk the five blocks to Sam's, and he did offer, so it's not like I'd be putting him out. I shrug at him. "If you're offering, that'd be great. I'm not going too far. Thank you, Sir." If Danny was here, he'd be driving me. I push that thought away.

The soldier nods at me. "No 'Sir' necessary. Jessie is fine—just don't tell any of the guys I let you call me that."

He winks at me. "Let me grab my shoes and my keys, and then I'll be ready."

"Where are you headed?" Uncle Dan asks from the couch, and I jump. The dude has super stealth or something. I didn't see him sitting there drinking his coffee. He's wearing PJ pants, and his stockinged feet are kicked up on the coffee table.

"Just going to see Sam. Time to get back to normal life. Big school day Monday."

His jaw twitches. "Routines are good for getting back on track, but, Hattie, don't put too much expectation on things feeling normal."

I want to scream at him, ask him how the heck he would know, but the truth is, they all know. They're soldiers—they have rough lives full of death and heartache.

I hate that he is probably right. Things might never feel normal again, but I at least have to try.

He gets up from the couch and walks around the coffee table to stand in front of me. These men all love and care about me, whether I appreciate it or not. Uncle Dan, especially—he's family, after all.

I look up into his pained blue eyes. "I love you, kid. I'm here if you need me."

"Thanks, Uncle Dan, you, too." My eyes burn with emotion, but I shake it off. Jessie rounds the corner, and I fly out the door after him without looking back. I have to keep moving, or I might just run back to the safety of my bed and stay there forever.

Jessie is driving a silver compact rental car—he flew in from Florida. He tells me all about it as I give him directions to Sam's house, so I am relieved when I see her barn-red house come into view and her car parked in the driveway. I probably should have called before I left, but I didn't want to give myself any more chances to back out. I need to see Sam and get back into the swing of my own life.

"Thanks again for the ride, Jessie. Do you know your way back?" I ask.

"Of course, I'm excellent with direction. Compliments of land nav training." He grins. The guy is sufferably friendly, which normally I would find sweet, but today I just want to get away from his cheerfulness.

Thanking him, I hop out, running up to Sam's front door without glancing back at Jessie's car. The gravel is wet, probably from the sprinklers, and I track mud on my sandals and up her front porch. I kick them off and lift my hand to knock as the door swings open.

"Thank God you're here!" Sam grabs my hand and pulls me into the house, her hands flailing in the air for dramatic emphasis. "I was getting ready to stage an intervention!"

I stare at my gorgeous and wild red-headed best friend and feel a real grin forming on my face. This is definitely where I am meant to be.

We spend most of the early afternoon just talking and hanging out in her bedroom. Sam is just glad to have me back, and I am thankful for her love of gossip for once. She's been catching me up on the two weeks of school

I have missed. I know she is dying to ask me about the drama at the funeral and what is happening with my mom, and I love her for holding herself back and giving me a few hours of normal. It isn't easy for Sam to let things stew—she's like a dog with a bone when there's gossip to be known. But, surprisingly, she stays quiet, pulling out the nail polish and getting to work painting my toes a gorgeous shade of black cherry.

"My mom is at the Fremont Hotel," I blurt out, and she stops painting mid-toe.

"You talked to her?" Her eyes are wide, her mouth hanging open in surprise.

"No, but I think I'm going to today. I want to see what she has to say..."

"I bet you broke her nose—that was a mean right hook!" Sam giggles, making a fist and pretending to swing at me.

"Oh my gosh. I really don't know where that came from!" I insist, and she just shakes her head.

"Wherever it came from, it was AWESOME! It happened so fast, or I bet someone would have gotten a good video of it for Instagram!" She goes back to painting my toes.

"I'm glad there's no video—can you imagine?"

"Yeah, I can; you'd be Insta-famous! Hashtag Mother-Daughter-brawl. It would be epic! Everyone's talking about it, anyway..." She trails off, looking at me from the side as if she's said too much.

"What else are they saying?" I'm not sure I want to know, but I don't want to take the words back once I've said them, either.

"Mostly, they just feel bad about everything. There are little shrines to Danny all over the school. People really loved him. They also think you're a total badass for going up there and telling your mom where to stick it." She finishes my toes and sits back to admire her work.

"Everyone did love him." I sigh, and her face softens.

"They love you, too, you know—we all do. We're all here for you, Hattie. I know you don't like to let people in, but you're easy to love." She shrugs and gets up to put her nail polish collection away, and I'm happy for the chance to collect myself. Sam always knows just what to say to get through to me; maybe that's why I've avoided her so hard. I wasn't ready before, but I'm coming around.

"Thanks for singing at the funeral, Sam. It was beautiful, and I'll never forget it." She sits down next to me, leaning her head on my shoulder.

"It was the least I could do. He was like the brother I never had. He definitely treated me like an extra-annoying little sister, and I am going to miss him, too." We both go silent, my mind playing out scenes of her and Danny bantering over the years. They were a comedic duo.

"He's missing you, too, wherever he is." I smile, and, for the first time, I feel like I truly believe what I've said.

20

Mommy Dearest

IT'S ALMOST DINNERTIME WHEN I ask Sam if she minds dropping me off at the Fremont Hotel. I've decided not to tell her that Dad is gone again—it has been a good day with plenty of heavy thoughts, so I can drop that bombshell later.

She agrees to drop me off as long as I promise to call her for a ride home when I'm finished. She thinks I should stay the night with her, and I am tempted to take her up on the offer. So far, I've felt a lot lighter being away from the heavy cloud that's hanging over my house.

I think about asking her to come inside with me but then quickly change my mind. This is my battle, and I want my mom to tell me what she really means and not think she has to pretend in front of Sam. I know Dad is always less harsh when there is an audience. This might be the only chance I ever get to know the truth.

Ready or not.

———— ♡ ♡ ♡ ————

The Fremont Hotel is the nicest hotel in our little town. It's smack dab in the middle, near the small shopping strip we call a mall. When you really want to go shopping, you have to make the one-hour drive to Waco, but this little area is nice. Treasures are always waiting to be found in the weird little shops here.

The hotel isn't very busy this time of year; it's hot, and no one wants to be this far off the beaten path. It's not like we're near Magnolia or anything worth making the stop for. At least McGregor has SpaceX if you're lucky enough to get a tour.

Only a handful of cars sit in the parking lot. I go through the double set of glass doors and look around the ornate lobby. I've always loved the big crystal chandelier that greets you from the high ceiling, making the light glitter all around like a fancy disco ball. They host some of our high school dances in this place. They have a gorgeous ballroom on the main floor that seems out of place in McKinley Lake, but none of us complain when we get to dance in style.

I walk up the long, red carpet to the reception area. A tall man in a business suit mans the desk, and he gives me a friendly smile. "Hello, Miss, how can I assist you tonight?" I'm thankful I don't recognize him, because that means he probably doesn't know who I am, either.

"I'm here to see my mother, but I forgot to write her room number down," I say, slapping my forehead and grinning at him. "She always says 'in one ear, out the other.' She's going to be really annoyed with me if I don't get up there soon—we're having a special girls' weekend."

"I'm sure we can figure it out, you and I." He types something on his computer. "What's the name, doll?"

"Nancy Tate," I answer, and then I wonder if she's still going by Tate after all these years. "Or Nancy Calloway, if she's mad at my dad. We're a family of comedians." I laugh, nervous I've already messed this up. I didn't want Dad to know I was coming here, so I hadn't asked him the room number. He might not have known it, and then he would have tried to call her. I didn't want to give her the chance to bolt. I want to catch her off guard. Dad has always said people are the most honest when they're not expecting you.

The clerk pauses for a second but then laughs. "She must be mad at dear old Dad then; it's under Calloway. Room 508, but you'll need a concierge key for that floor." He does a few things behind the counter and hands me a key card.

"Thank you. I appreciate your help, Sir!" I rush to the elevator before he sees how nervous I am and changes his mind.

I punch the number for the fifth floor and slide the concierge key into the reader. Should have guessed she'd be on the fancy floor. The ground spins, and I try to take deep breaths, muttering to myself in the empty elevator. "You can do this." I breathe. I close my eyes and will myself to feel Danny here with me. It doesn't work, but thinking of Danny gives me the last push that I need. I open my eyes as the elevator dings and walk out with purpose.

I find room 508 quickly and force myself to knock before I lose the nerve I've just built up. I hear someone on the other side of the door, and then it opens. The woman who answers looks so much like me, it's almost unnerving. Her nose is bruised and swollen, and both her eyes are black. I did that. It's hard not to feel a little smug.

She looks startled to see me, and I consider that point number two for me. She didn't anticipate this visit—maybe she even made an agreement with Dad to stay away from me.

"Henrietta, I'm surprised to see you." Her eyes narrow at me—she probably expects me to throw more punches. I hold my hands up, palms out in surrender, as I look her over. She looks like she's going somewhere fancy. She has black slacks and a white silk blouse on, and her heels are a mile high.

"I just want to talk." I put my hands down, and she steps back, opening the door and allowing me to enter. "And I go by Hattie now."

Her room is large and ultra-fancy; it must cost a fortune to stay here. There are two plush purple chairs that have golden feet and a white love seat situated around an ornate coffee table. To the left is a wet bar with a couple of high-backed bar stools. To the right, the bedroom door is open, and a giant bed covered in pillows sits next to a spa tub. I sit on one of the purple chairs and cross my muddy sandals.

"Hattie, yes," she murmurs. "Your dad never did like the idea of naming you Henrietta; he said it was an old lady's name." She sits across from me on the love seat, crossing her legs elegantly at the ankle. Her high heels look intimidating.

She should remember this, but I explain it anyway. "Actually, Danny came up with it. I guess Henrietta was too much of a mouthful for a toddler." I try to smile, but the memories burn. He should be here, too. He should be the one getting his questions answered, but since he can't ask them, I will do it for him.

"Would you like something to drink?" Mom asks. "There are some sodas in the mini-fridge." She gestures toward the minibar, but I shake my head. I don't intend to stay here that long.

An awkward silence falls between us, and I'm not sure what to say. I should have planned out some questions before barging in here unannounced. I try to think of the questions Danny mentioned when we'd talked about her. I wonder if I should take a gentle approach, but then words fall out of my mouth. "Why did you leave?"

Her eyebrows shoot up, and then she quickly recovers. "Direct, I appreciate that." She uncrosses her legs and leans forward, elbows on her knees. "I left because I didn't like motherhood. It didn't suit me. Your father, he was a natural parent, always worried about every little thing. I didn't have those concerns. I wanted to go out, see my friends, travel. When I met your dad and found out who he was, I was thrilled by the idea of an adventurous life. For the first little while, it was: We moved to Europe then Hawaii..." She trails off, her eyes seeing things that I can't.

I stare at her. Of all the things I expected her to say, I hadn't thought selfishness would be her response. I had expected apologies, excuses.

"When we found out we were having twins, things immediately changed. Your dad took it upon himself to ask for a stability extension so we wouldn't get moved around for a few years. I felt doubly shackled. I know that's hard to hear, but I just felt horrified by the idea that my children were keeping me from an exciting life." She shrugs like she just told me she doesn't like pineapple on pizza.

I shift uncomfortably in my chair. "So you left because you wanted more adventure..." I repeat. Looking her over, I note her perfectly manicured nails, her hair wrapped in a fancy twist again, not a single strand out of place. I see the diamonds on her wrists, her neck, and her ears, but none on her ring finger. Everything about her screams expensive taste and pampering. "Do you work?" I ask, wondering how she affords it all. Dad makes good money, but he's worked his whole life to get where he is.

"Oh, I do, and I don't. I have a lot of rich friends who like to pamper me." She smiles to herself. "Male friends. You could, too, someday with a face like yours."

A face almost identical to hers, she means, and she is a beautiful woman, but it doesn't exactly feel like a compliment. I feel sick. She left Dad so she could have a bunch of rich male friends? So she wouldn't be "shackled" by a loving family? "Did you love us?" I ask, and I hate that it comes out sounding like a plea. I hate that I suddenly care how she answers.

She sighs, leaning back into the sofa again. "I guess I did, in my own way. I thought I loved your father, but I think I just loved that he loved me. He worshiped me in those early years. When I left, I thought I might miss him and regret my choice, but I just moved on, easy as pie. I loved the two of you kids enough to leave you with him. He was better for you than I'd have been. I only regret sticking around for so long."

Finally, something I agree with. Dad was better for us—he's been a wonderful dad, considering. Maybe he hasn't been around as much as we would have liked, but he was working during all those times, trying to give us the best life we could have. He didn't just run away. I mean, he'd just left me again, and though I am really disappointed, I am also proud of him, if I am being honest. He sticks by his commitments, always.

"Why did you come to the funeral?" I finally ask the one question that's completely mine. I am not sure if I should ask it, afraid the answer might be the final breaking point. I feel cold despite the heat of the night—maybe I should call this woman the Ice Queen.

"I saw coverage on the news, and then Danny's face was all over Facebook and Instagram. It was so strange—it was like seeing your dad again. I was angry, too, that he'd let something happen to one of you. He was supposed to be the better parent." She makes a face, and I'm tempted to punch her again. Did she not learn anything at the funeral?

I sit on my hands to keep myself from doing anything rash. "So you came to yell at Dad?"

"Of course not. That wouldn't change anything. I wanted to know what happened, and the news was saying terrible things about me. Someone told a reporter I was a deadbeat mother, as if that's even a thing. I wanted to clear the air. I also wanted to see you, to see if you'd like to come with me. I'm going to stay in Dallas for awhile since I came all this way. Although, that was before you assaulted me."

"I am sorry I hit you. I'm not usually a violent person—you just happened to catch me on one of the worst days of my life." I smirk. I'm not actually sorry, but Dad did teach me some manners.

"All that fiery passion, I thought for a second we might have something in common. You apologizing for your actions, though, has your dad written all over it. We are women—we have to take what we want and be unapologetic about it." She throws her hands up, clearly exasperated.

My anger has begun to dissipate, and, in its stead, I only feel disappointment. I want to feel touched that she wants to take me to Dallas and spend time with me, but I don't. I don't feel any affection for this woman who birthed me. Yes, we may look nearly identical, but I know without a doubt that I am more like my father in every way. This woman isn't capable of loving anyone but herself.

I always thought Nana and Dad were just bitter, that they'd overexaggerated her selfishness. Even if *selfish* was the wrong word to describe her, it was much closer than *maternal,* which is the opposite of what she is.

I came here thinking we could hash it out and maybe she'd have some reasonable explanation for leaving us and never looking back. She doesn't, though—no postpartum depression story, not an affair or a scandal; she just didn't want us. She hasn't even apologized once, and judging by her "women don't apologize" comment, I don't think I'll ever get one out of her.

Standing up, I wipe my palms on my shorts. "Danny always wanted to meet you—I think that's what made me come here tonight. He always wanted to ask you questions, but after hearing your answers, or lack thereof, I know in my bones he was better off for never getting them." Turning, I head for the door. "I'm so glad he never did this."

"You're just like your father," I hear her say. "You think you're better because you care about family over everything else. Some of us just have different priorities."

I stop in my tracks for a split second. Her comment sends a trickle of fury over every inch of my body. For a moment, I stop to consider what our lives would have been like with her in them. Would we have been different kids? Would we have stayed in McKinley Lake? Would Danny have grown up playing baseball instead of football? Would he have even been on the field that night? Would he still be alive today? Her *priorities* could have been the reason for his demise. It was hard to stop myself from going down that rabbit hole.

"You might look like me, but you'll never be my daughter," she adds, and my hand stills before it gets to the doorknob.

Her words are snarky and meant to hurt me, but they make me smile; I'm glad she can't see any similarities between us. Later, when all this soaks in, I might feel sad, but right now, I'm just angry and need to get out of here. Comparing me to Dad is probably the nicest compliment she's ever given out, so I focus on that.

"Thank you," I mumble under my breath and open the door. How ironic the last words I'll ever say to her are the two she deserves the least. I don't stop walking as I exit; I just head out the door and down to the lobby. I don't know if she will try to follow me, but I doubt it.

I'm glad I came. If anything, I know now that everything Nana ever told me was true. Dad just had the unfortunate luck of falling in love with a woman incapable of returning his affection. I wish I could have seen Dad before that woman in there broke him.

My body is shaking hard with adrenaline, and the last thing I want to do is call Sam for a ride right now. It was really good talking with her earlier, but now I feel like a ticking time bomb. I need to breathe, walk this off. My mind is racing, and my heart can't quite catch up with all that's going through my head. I meant what I said; I'm beyond glad that Danny never met that woman. Part of me would like to go back and really tell her how I feel, but it wouldn't accomplish anything.

The lobby is deserted, and that's fine by me. I toss the keycard on the desk as I pass it and head for the exit. It's less than a mile to the local coffee shop, and I have nothing but time to burn.

21

Caffeine Confessions

THE COFFEE SHOP LIGHTS are a bright beacon down the street. The brick corner building is alive with activity—I see people shuffling in and out of the doors as I approach. All the daylight has faded, and darkness permeates everything that the streetlights don't touch. It's after nine on a Saturday night, but that doesn't seem to deter the caffeine junkies. On a normal Saturday, Danny and I would probably catch a movie before we'd be caught somewhere boring like Jazz Beans, but my legs keep pushing me toward the door anyway.

The building is old, an original part of downtown McKinley Lake. The windows are small and frosted with age, but the bricks are hearty, and the chandeliers are original and glorious. Sometimes I get a coffee or tea and sit in the back with a book and read for hours. My hands itch for the comfort of a good book.

The door swings out into the frigid night air, the bell above twinkling as it bangs against the wood. "Good evening." An elderly man smiles, holding the door open for me. I nod at him and step through.

"Thank you, Sir," I say, shuffling into the inviting air-conditioning of the coffee shop. Inside are plenty of open overstuffed couches and chairs in varying shades of blue. The floor is old and wooden. The tables are all glossy white with a single candle flickering on each one, and the light bounces off every surface like twinkling Christmas lights. It's like a time warp here—everything looks old and charming. The familiar smell of coffee calms my nerves.

The counter is straight ahead, and the line is short. Even though it seemed busy from outside, it's actually pretty deserted inside. I order an iced vanilla chai latte and a blueberry muffin and find a seat in the back corner against the wall, an excellent seat for people watching while I drink my tea. I'm not sure exactly what I'm doing, but maybe if I just sit for awhile, I'll figure it out. I pull my phone from my back pocket, placing it on the table as I settle into my chair.

Holding the cup in my hands, I sip the icy liquid. I let it cool me through to my bones as I survey the coffee shop. A couple by the front door looks like they're on a date. He keeps leaning in and touching her forearm with his fingertips, and she blushes at him each time. The barista has changed the music to soft country, and when Rascal Flatts starts belting out a love song and he finally links his fingers with hers, she beams.

My eyes burn a little, and I shake it off. Life goes on. The world isn't going to stop because Danny is gone, and it shouldn't. I don't want anyone else to feel this crushing pain that I feel, either. I wish things could be different. I wish kids never died.

Heartache is heavy, and as much as I'm still torn about everything, if I'm truly honest with myself, there's only one person I want here with me right now. I reach across the table for my phone and shoot a quick text before I can lose my nerve.

The bell above the coffee shop door jingles, and I watch as he comes in from the sticky night air. His dark hair is disheveled, and his head swivels around looking for me, his forehead creased with worry. He's wearing light blue jeans with holes in the knees and his football sweatshirt. He's overdressed for the balmy weather, and I wonder what I've pulled him from on a Saturday night.

He sees me then, and his face softens, the slightest smile touching his lips before he takes long, confident strides over to my table. "Hattie." He sits across from me, his eyes finding mine and holding my gaze.

My heartbeat quickens like it always does when he looks at me like that, and warmth creeps into my face. I'm not sure I'll ever get used to him looking at me this way. "Hey, Kellan." Now that he's here, I hope I'm brave enough to say everything that's on my mind. My palms are clammy from holding my cup, and my tongue feels too big for my mouth. We didn't exactly leave things on good terms at the funeral.

"What's up? I got your text and rushed over. Everything okay?" He reaches out and puts a hand over mine on the table, and I stare at it. It's such a simple, sweet gesture, but I still feel the electricity from his touch. It burns into my skin like a brand, but I don't pull away. He's already made the first move—I have to stop running.

"I wanted to see you."

He swallows but doesn't say anything, and the silence weighs heavily between us. He traces the back of my hand with his thumb and waits patiently. Watching his long fingers is hypnotic; I have to bite my lip and force myself to continue.

"I went and saw my mom like you suggested," I tell him. His thumb stills, but he doesn't move his hand away. This isn't exactly what I want to talk to him about, but it's a start. "Turns out, she's worse than I imagined, but I guess it does feel better to just know." I shrug.

"I'm sorry, Hattie. It really wasn't my place to say anything."

I wave off his apology. He was just being a good friend; he doesn't owe me an explanation. Besides, that's not why I've called him here. I take another deep breath. "It's okay, you were right. I needed to face my fear and just get to the truth."

"She's an idiot if she doesn't see what she's missed out on... you don't need her, anyway." He squeezes my hand lightly and smiles, his dimple flashing. My heart leaps at his words, and I smile back.

"Yeah, I pretty much told her so." I grin back, and we both laugh.

"Was there something else you wanted to talk about?" His voice is low and quiet and sounds slightly husky. He looks nervous, and I wonder if he's guessed what I have to say.

"I need to apologize. I've been selfish and awful. I know I've been really crazy lately, all over the place. Like I told you the other day, I'm still not sure from one moment to the next what I'm going to do or feel or say."

"You're forgiven. I was harsh—I didn't mean to say those things to you..."

I squeeze his fingers. "What I do know, Kellan, is that I can't ignore this thing between us for another minute. I already lost Danny, and my heart can't take anymore right now. I just want you close to me. I can't keep pretending that I can just ignore this because Danny didn't like it. I can't stop thinking about you... about us." My words come out in a rush, but they feel right.

Kellan stills, his smile falters, and he clears his throat. "Are you sure, Hattie? I've been trying to respect your choice to stay away, but it hasn't been easy." He runs his free hand through his hair and lets out a shuddering breath.

I know it's not fair to him the way I've been pushing and pulling, kissing him and then asking him to back off. I deserve this reserved response. I just feel like he's the one thing that can hold me together. Sure, I'm terrified this could all blow up in our faces and I could lose him, too, but the way things are now, I don't have him, anyway. I don't want to have regrets, don't want to pretend that he doesn't feel like the happiest part of my world.

"I'm sure, Kellan." I squeeze his hand and look at his full lips, praying he'll try to kiss me again. I crave the contact, the promise that it holds.

"God, Hattie." He breaks eye contact and lets go of me to bury his face in his hands. He looks so tortured, and suddenly I'm worried I'm too late. Maybe he's changed his mind now; maybe I've pushed him away too many times. I wouldn't even be able to blame him. That day in Danny's room, I'd practically shoved him out the window and told him to stay out of my life. This whole thing with Mom, Dad leaving again, Danny... this is the one thing I actually have some control over. I'm admitting I have these feelings, and I don't want to fight them anymore. This is the one bright spot in the darkest time of my life. He is the light.

"Kellan, I'm really sorry..." I start to apologize, but I choke on my own emotions.

In an instant, he's in front of me, squatting down so that we're at eye level. "I thought I'd have to find a way to let you go, too." He brushes my windblown hair behind my ears with shaking hands. "I lost my best friend, and I don't know which way is up right now. I'm like a walking fumble. The only thing I know for sure is that I want to hold you, talk to you, be next to you. I'm crazy about you, Hattie."

Electricity crackles between us. The truth is out in the open now, and I can feel it adding fuel to the fire. I lean forward, my lips parted slightly, my eyes falling closed as I smell his body wash and his skin, and then his velvet lips brush mine, and I hear myself sigh. My hands find their way into his hair and hold him to me. Our kisses are soft and slow and devastatingly tender—I feel all of my reservations drain out through my toes, and, for once, I just let myself fall.

We make out in the coffee shop for awhile, both of us too afraid to break the spell. I feel a fevered calm that I didn't know was possible. His hands are in my hair, and mine are wrapped snugly around his neck. We are holding onto each other like life preservers in the midst of a storm, giving the couple by the window a run for their money.

This storm has been a hurricane. I never should have tried to fight these feelings, because right here, in this moment, I believe things might actually feel good again. Not fixed—nothing could take away that ache for Danny—but my world is a little less shaky, and that is a start.

Someone coughs, and we break contact to look up. One of the coffee shop employees is standing near our table with a mop bucket. "Sorry to interrupt the young lovers"—the gray-haired lady tsks at us—"but it's just about time to close up."

Kellan and I both laugh. "Thank you, ma'am," he drawls. "Have a great night." I slip my phone back in my pocket and take Kellan's hand. We rush out into the cool night together.

Kellan's truck is parked around the corner in the small lot with only two other cars—the darkness is only broken up by the streetlamp a few feet away. Kellan unlocks the doors to his truck and starts the engine with his remote starter. I glance at my phone—it's just after ten. Sam sent me a text thirty minutes ago asking if I was okay, so I quickly type a message telling her I am out for coffee but nothing more. She will want a play-by-play, and I don't want to ruin the magic.

Somewhere in the back of my mind, I feel a little guilty for feeling this good. Danny hasn't even been gone that long, and here I am finding something special with his best friend.

"Hey, you good?" Kellan comes around and tips my chin up, forcing me to look into those dark eyes.

"Yeah, just thinking about Danny," I say honestly, biting my lip, emotions churning forward. He guides me into the truck, and I sit, still watching his face.

"Yeah, me, too." He sighs and shuts the door. I watch him walk around the truck and then climb inside. He doesn't reach behind for his seatbelt, just puts his hands on the wheel and stares quietly into the night.

"What are you thinking?" I want to know, but I'm also afraid of his answer. What if it's Kellan's turn to regret his choices? I've done my fair share of back and forth—I wouldn't blame him if he started questioning things, too.

"I miss him—it's so weird to not just have him around." He drums the steering wheel with his fingertips. "There are so many things I want to tell him, and then I remember I can't."

I nod because my throat is choking up, and I blink back the start of tears.

He nods back. "I just... I think about all the crazy shit we did together. The dumb fights, the diabolical pranks..."

I laugh at that one. Those two were definitely a pair of troublemakers. Kellan leans back against his seat and turns the air-conditioning up. We're both flushed, but I doubt the AC can fix this feeling. He turns on the radio, and country music plays softly in the background. It's all so normal and comfortable, like we've been doing this for years. I suppose we have, just with other people around. Other than kissing, not much is different about how we are around each other. I'm still nervous and want to stare at him, only now I see that his attraction to me is more than wishful thinking on my part.

"Do you feel him with you, Kellan?"

"Yes... maybe that's wild, but I do. I feel like he's sticking close, keeping his eyes on me."

Jealousy threatens to strangle me with its big, green hands. I try to tell myself that maybe I don't feel Danny with me because Kellan needs him more right now, but I'd give anything to feel that connection. I haven't felt him near me once since he left, no matter how hard I try, and I wonder if I ever will. The closest I've gotten is reading the words from his journals, feeling like he is sharing them with me.

Thinking of his journals sparks something inside me, and I feel a plan forming. "Want to do something crazy?" I ask.

"I'll do anything for you, Hattie." His words are serious, but I catch him winking at me. It makes me smile.

"Did you leave that ladder up in the backyard?"

Kellan eyes me. "Uh, yes... why?"

"We're going to sneak into Danny's room like you guys used to. I want to show you something." I should have thought of this sooner.

22

Brotherly Blessings

TRYING MY BEST TO hold back a giggle, I climb the ladder to Danny's window. Kellan waits below, shushing me. We didn't take long to get here, and we were careful and parked a street over so we wouldn't alert anyone in the house of our presence.

It's still early, so I doubt Melissa and Uncle Dan have gone to bed yet. No way Uncle Dan would let me be alone with Kellan at night, but that's exactly what I want. Just the two of us, snuggled up together in Danny's closet, reading his words and feeling like we're all together again, if only for a moment.

I wiggle the window the way Kellan instructed, and it comes open with ease. I laugh quietly as I climb through the opening. I love the thought of them doing this night after night and never getting caught. I imagine Dad probably knows all about this and just pretends not to. He's too smart and well-trained to have missed all the signs.

Kellan climbs in after me and closes the window behind us. The room is warm and dark; the only light is from the moonlight shining through the window.

The familiar smell of my brother envelopes me and greets me like a hug. The door is locked—just how I left it—and the bathroom door is shut as well. Everyone seems to be respecting my wishes for it to stay untouched.

I hear sounds from the TV down the hall and muffled conversation. We will have to be very quiet to avoid being discovered. The last thing I want to do to a postwar soldier is surprise him.

I place a finger over my lips and then point to Danny's closet, and Kellan follows my directions. I move stealthily to my room to retrieve the journal I've stashed under my pillow. It's dark, but I know the terrain by heart, so it's painless and silent. I close the bathroom door behind me and then join Kellan in the closet.

The closet seems so much smaller with the two of us packed inside, but I turn on the light and remove my sandals. Kellan is sitting on the floor with his back leaned up against the wall, clothes brushing the top of his head. He's taken off his sweatshirt and is using it as a pillow behind his head. He looks so handsome: hair messed up, black t-shirt pulling tight over his muscled body, dark eyes searching my face for clues about what I have planned. I smile at him, and it earns me a flash of that dimple I love.

"I'm glad you came. I wanted you to see this." I hold the yellow notebook out to him, and he takes it from me gently.

His eyebrows quirk up, and he swallows hard. "Is this one of his secret books?"

I sit beside him, snuggling up close. He lifts an arm and squeezes me to his warm body. I rest my head on his shoulder and open the notebook, flipping through the first few pages that I've already read.

"It is. I know it might be wrong to read his private journals, but it makes me feel like I'm talking with him. I wanted to share that with someone. No, not just with someone..." My voice shakes. "With you."

He nods, kissing my forehead softly, his grip on my body tightening. "Thank you, Hattie. For letting me in."

We spend the next few hours whisper-reading Danny's words to each other. The time seems to fly by, and soon the house goes silent. We make it through three journals, all dated months and some even years ago. I love learning silly thoughts and beautiful poems that came from my brother's mind. They scream Danny, and with each one, my heart feels a little less heavy. I will cherish these books for the rest of my life; I already know it.

Kellan is mostly quiet unless he's reading, but I can tell it's helping him, too. He hasn't let go of me since we snuggled up, and I feel warm and comforted in his arms.

I reach for another journal and open the front. The date is more recent, only a week before the start of school. Goosebumps prickle on my arms making the hair stand up.

School starts next week! Me and Kel are going to take the team all the way! I can already taste the victory!

We went to the lake again. You should see the girls this year—I don't know what they did over the summer, but they are all looking confident and hot! I want to ask Sarah out, but I think I'll wait until we win the first game of the season. That always makes me feel invincible.

Kellan and Hattie are doing that weird oblivious flirting thing again. It freaks me out still because Hattie feels like my responsibility. I know there's no one better than Kel, but I'm just not ready to see my sister suck face... especially with my best friend.

Uncle Dan called—he's thinking about asking his girlfriend to marry him, and he wanted to know if I'd want to be a groomsman. He really wanted to know if I thought Dad would want to be his best man. It's funny; they'd die for each other without question, but they act like they feel physical pain when it comes to sharing their feelings or asking for favors. I hope I don't act like that when I'm older, but I think I already do. Oh well... if you can't beat 'em, join 'em!

Danny knew before both of us that we were getting serious, and it figures. He's always been able to read me like a book.

I'm happy for Uncle Dan. I wish he would have confided in me, too, but he's always had a closer bond with Danny. I think Melissa is great for him. I'll have to help Dad come to the same conclusion.

I lean back to see Kellan's reaction and realize he's fallen asleep. He looks so peaceful, so I decide not to disturb him. I just snuggle in and turn the page.

Well, it finally happened. Kellan straight-up admitted he's looking at Hattie as more than my sister. I panicked and pulled the Bro card, reminding him she's way off-limits. I thought he was going to fight me a little harder, but I did threaten to get Dad involved.

Hahaha—you should have seen the look on his face. I should have taken a picture and put it on Instagram with the caption: "That face you make when you crap your pants." The thing is, the more I think about it, the more I'm okay with the idea. They've always had a weird flirty thing going on, and really, he knows I'll kill him if he hurts her. I can't think of a single dude that would treat her as well as Kel would. I need to suck it up and just come clean, let him know I won't stand in his way if Hattie wants to date him. I mean, it still feels super gross, but... I want her to be happy, and it should be her choice, not mine.

Hattie and I had a huge fight, and I feel like garbage about it. Maybe I should talk to them both after this whole first game of the season is behind me and I can concentrate again. She thinks I want to control her, but I don't. She's so frustrating. I love her and want to protect her, but she sees it as some caveman thing. I don't actually blame her for feeling that way, but it's not because she's a girl. I think she's tougher than me, to be honest. It's because she means more to me than anyone. I wish I'd just said that.

Her tears killed me, though. I can be such an idiot.

My cheeks are wet with tears as I finish the entry, and I brush them away before they can fall on the pages and smear the ink. The fight we had that Tuesday before the game had been weighing on him as much as it weighed on me. He was okay with the idea of me and Kellan, and he was going to tell me all of that before... before everything came crashing down and the world took him from us. I've been holding it together pretty well, but with Kellan's arm around me and the soft rise and fall of his chest lulling me to relax, I feel the cracks in my defenses.

To distract myself from the pain, I try to remember the stages of grief we learned in school.

Number one, Denial and Isolation.

I definitely hit that one more than once in the last week.

Number two, Anger.

Ask my mom's face if I hit that one or not.

Number three, Bargaining.

I think I skipped three and went straight to four.

Depression.

I'm still here at four, and I don't know if I'll ever get out.

Step five is Acceptance.

For some reason, I think if I ever make it that far, that'll be the worst. How can I accept that my brother is gone forever? I'd rather live back at step one.

Danny's words ring in my head. *I do want her to be happy...*

I'm trying, Danny. I want to make you proud.

I close my eyes and imagine Danny asking me to watch *Teen Wolf* in his room, popcorn filled to the brim of his bowl, him perched upon his throne of pillows. I see his eyes crinkled in laughter as we make jokes about the bromance between the characters or when I accuse him of only watching the show for the hot actresses. I can feel him covering my eyes with his hands when one of the hot guys takes off his shirt. I hear his voice telling me to pause it so he can refill the snacks, because, as much as he hates to admit it, he doesn't want to miss a second of the drama. If anything, he's more obsessed with the show than I have ever been, but he'd never admit it. The memory wraps around my heart like a cocoon, and I embrace its warmth, holding on to this moment with all that I have.

23

Breaking News

SOMEONE IS YELLING, AND I shake myself awake. It takes me a minute to remember where I am, but then I do, and a smile touches my lips as I feel Kellan stir beside me. We must have fallen asleep on the floor of Danny's closet last night. The light is still on, and the notebooks are scattered across the floor. I'm still tucked tightly to Kellan's side, and I wonder if we moved at all while we slept.

Reluctantly, I slip out of his hold and stand up, cracking the closet door. I listen to the voices and try to make out what's happening in the house. With all the transient soldiers coming and going, it's not too unusual to have drama and noise in the mornings.

The voices are muffled and hard to understand, but I hear some alarming words come through. "... an attack on the forward operating base... unaccounted for... can't get a hold of Hattie..." Bile rises in my throat, but I try to contain my growing sense of panic. I drop to my knees and shake Kellan awake.

"Hattie?" he asks sleepily. "What time is it?" I reach in my pocket for my phone; I only vaguely remember shutting it off. I power it on and shake my head.

"I'm not sure, but I think something is wrong," I whisper back. My hands shake, and Kellan seems to finally wake up. He takes his own phone out of his pocket and shows me the lock screen. It's after ten in the morning, and he has six missed calls. We share twin looks of concern, and I shiver from the dread flooding my body. *Nothing more, please, Universe, I can't take anything else.*

So much for skipping that Bargaining stage.

My phone finally powers on, and I see I've missed sixteen calls and have multiple text messages. Uncle Dan has been trying to call me, and Sam has texted me over a dozen times.

I open her chat bubble:

> Sam: **Hattie??!! WHERE THE HECK ARE YOU??**

> Sam: **HATTTTTTIIIIEEEE...**

> Sam: **Your uncle keeps calling here and asking where you are.**

Sam: **I thought you were with your mom??**

Sam: **I called the hotel—your mom already checked out. Did something happen??**

Sam: **Are you with her now??**

Sam: **I think you better call soon...**

Sam: **Are you with Kellan?!?!?! I tried calling him, too, and no answer...**

Sam: **Hattie!!! Your uncle is gonna call the damn police! Call someone!**

I type a quick reply:

Me: **I'm home. I will call ASAP.**

Knowing Sam, she's pacing and plotting my murder for making her stress like this—once she's sure no one has harmed me, that is. I feel guilty for giving her the slip last night, but I know I can make it up to her with my juicy gossip: I spent the night with Kellan.

Panic closes in on me, and I make an apologetic face at Kellan. "I know this doesn't seem fair, but I think I have to shove you out the window again."

Pain flashes in those deep brown eyes, and even though I know that I need to hurry, I pull him to me by the fabric of his shirt and seal my lips to his. I let my hands slide into his hair, and I feel his hands seal me to him, pressing on the small of my back. It's heavenly, and now that I feel like I have Danny's blessing, I let myself fully enjoy the taste of his mouth, the feel of his hands, the electric buzz that shoots through me from head to toe.

Someone bangs on Danny's door, and I remember myself. "Hurry! I'll call you as soon as I can," I whisper to Kellan, and he looks slightly reassured from our kiss. He pecks my forehead, grabs his discarded sweatshirt, and rushes back out the window into the still morning air.

Turning off Danny's closet light, I step out into the bedroom. I stare at the door, the only thing protecting me from the news on the other side and force myself to move. With shaking hands, I unlock the door and pull it open.

Uncle Dan is midway down the hall, a phone pressed tightly to his ear, his fingers white from the pressure. He's wearing his company shirt and black slacks, and he looks all business except for his bare feet. When he hears the door, his entire body jerks back in my direction. "Thank God, we found her. Sorry to bother you... yes, I'll tell her." He ends the call and stalks toward me.

"Where the hell have you been?" he growls. His eyes search my body and then come back to my face when he finds me intact.

"I'm sorry. I fell asleep in Danny's closet, and I guess my phone was off." I shrug. It's the truth even if it's not the entire story. "Is something wrong?"

His face softens, and he scrubs a hand over his jaw before he responds. "I don't want you to panic, so let's have a seat in the living room and talk. We will discuss your whereabouts and activities from last night later." I'm still wearing yesterday's clothes, and I can see the questions in his eyes.

Melissa is waiting in the living room in Dad's chair. When she sees me, her face lights up with surprise. "Oh, thank heavens, where was she?" She speaks only to Dan, not meeting my eyes.

"Later," Uncle Dan says firmly, sitting on the couch and patting the seat next to him. "Sit."

I do as I'm told, crossing the room and folding my legs under me on the couch. I think something bad is coming, and I want to be comfortable. I don't want to run away this time. I will not be like my mother.

"Your dad was headed to the forward operating base in a remote region of Iraq. We aren't sure if he made it there or if he's still in transit—communication has been blacked out for safety. There was a rocket attack, and several soldiers and civilian contractors are unaccounted for. It was a heavy attack; buildings have come down, and they expect casualties.

"He caught a space-available flight out of Fort Hood, so there isn't a paper trail to follow. No one can tell me anything helpful right now, but I didn't want you to hear it from anyone but me." His face is serious, chiseled from stone, and shows no emotion. His training has kicked in, and he's giving away nothing.

The door to my heart feels like it's being pummeled. The battering ram is back in full force, and there's nowhere to hide. My first instinct is to run away, but I clasp my hands together and hold strong. I am Henrietta June Tate, daughter of Joseph Emerson Tate, retired Sergeant Major of the US Army. I have been preparing for a moment like this my entire life. I can hold this family together, even if I am the last man standing.

I look at Uncle Dan square in the eyes. "I refuse to lose another member of this family. You will let me know the second you hear something; am I clear?" I hear Melissa gasp. She's twisting her hair around her fingers nervously, and now she's looking at me like I've lost my marbles completely. She's probably not used to young girls standing up to strong men or giving them orders.

He nods at me. "Yes, ma'am, you have my word."

I have phone calls to make, but as strong as I am attempting to be, I need a moment alone before all the tears start leaking out of me. Keeping my head high, I stand up from the couch.

"Oh—and Hattie?" Uncle Dan catches my gaze and holds it. "We love you."

24

Phone a Friend

ONCE I'M SAFELY TUCKED in my room, I call Sam first. I know she's probably really worried and equally pissed off. I left her hanging, and that goes against the first rule of sisterhood.

The line rings twice before she answers. "This had better be good."

"Sam, I'm really sorry..."

"Just skip the apologies and get to the good stuff before I block your number and ghost you." She demands it, but I hear the worry in her voice. I'm afraid if I talk about Dad, I'll break into a sob fest, so I start at the beginning.

"I talked to my mom—turns out, she's just straight evil. I'm not talking about Disney evil, either—more like *Game of Thrones* evil. Calling her Queen of the Evil Stepmothers would be a demotion for her. I feel like I have closure now, though, so I can live the rest of my life no longer wondering what I'm missing."

"Oh geez, was it horrible? Why didn't you call me? I said I'd come get you!" Sam cries, but she's intrigued now, and the anger has left her tone.

"I was going to, but I needed to walk it off first. I was angry and sad for Danny, maybe even a little sad for me. I went to Jazz Beans to get a chai latte."

"And then what? Because according to your scary uncle, you never came home last night... you'd better start spilling the good stuff." I hear her nails clicking on her phone impatiently and smile. I love this girl's antics and attitude so much, and I'm really thankful she puts up with my crap.

"I met with Kellan." I don't need to pause for dramatic effect, but I do pause to bask in the memory of our coffee date.

"You *what*? Oh my gosh, tell me everything."

I go on for a while, gushing over Kellan and telling Sam all about the electric kissing sessions and the night we spent snuggled up together in Danny's closet. I leave out the part about what Danny's journals say—I want Kellan to be the first one I talk to about all of that. I really need to call him, too, but I'm thankful for the distraction that gushing about the boy I like has given me.

"... and then I heard Uncle Dan making all this noise in the house, and I realized something was up. I'm so sorry I had my phone off. I should have just set it to vibrate last night."

Sam grows quiet, and I mirror her silence. The air grows heavy as the reality of the present situation descends upon me.

"Are you ready to tell me what was so urgent that he called everyone you know looking for you?" she asks quietly.

"Sergeant Dad left yesterday morning to head overseas... and there's been a rocket attack. No one knows where he is," I say in a rush. Better to get it out before I choke on the words. "We're in blackout mode now, so we just have to wait and see." I feel tears burn in the back of my throat, and I ignore them. I cannot keep breaking down—how much crying can a person do, anyway? I'm so dehydrated by now that I'll probably turn to dust at any moment.

"I'm coming over," Sam says, and I nod at the phone as if she can see me. We end the call, and I sit on the edge of my bed trying to catch my breath. I hope with everything I have that Dad is okay.

I feel an overwhelming sense of regret with how we left things. Dad was trying, and I ran away as usual. I didn't even say goodbye. I really need to stop doing that.

After washing my face and composing myself, I call Kellan's number. Other than random text messages, we haven't talked on the phone on more than a few occasions. Usually, it's me asking where the heck Danny is and if he could please send him home for dinner. The thought brings so many memories to mind.

Kellan picks up before it even has a chance to ring. "What is it, Hattie? Is everything okay?"

"I don't know... Nothing is confirmed, but there was an attack on the base where Dad was supposed to be, and, as of now, he's unaccounted for. Sam is coming over, and all we can really do is wait..." I want to ask him to come, too, but I don't want to overwhelm him with my family stuff. I know he's suffering, too.

"I'll be right there. I called my mom and let her know where I was, but I've just been sitting in my truck worried about you. I'm two streets over, right where we parked last night. Warn whoever you need to, but I'm coming." I laugh a little. He's so sweet, and I can't believe I ever tried to push him away.

"Kel?" I ask quietly. "Maybe just use the front door this time."

25

Hurry Up and Wait

OUR HOUSE IS FULL of chatter and nervous energy. Uncle Dan ordered pizzas when my friends showed up, and we have been playing board games—Sam and Kellan just started a very competitive game of cards. No one has touched the food, and any time a phone makes a noise, we all jump.

I know that when a soldier is killed in action, they send a car to tell the families, but that doesn't extend to the families of civilian contractors. We will get a phone call one way or another. I still catch myself peeking out the main window and watching for headlights, anyway. Military brat reflex.

Melissa is pretending to read a book from Dad's chair. I know she's not actually reading because she hasn't turned a single page in the hours that we've been sitting here.

Kellan is still wearing his clothes from yesterday, and his black t-shirt is wrinkled from sleep. His hair is mussed up from running his hands through it, but he still looks ridiculously handsome. Sam yells when Kellan makes a winning move; she throws him an icy glare, and his dimple flashes when he shrugs at her.

If it were any other day, this would look like a fun, casual party at the Tate house.

Sam keeps sneaking glances at me. Her red hair is pulled into a pony, and she has jean shorts and a tank top on. She's dressed casually, but her expression is all business. I think she expects me to snap at any moment, and she acts like she's afraid if she asks how I'm doing, she'll send me over the edge.

I'm tired, but I'd had the presence of mind to change into jeans and a hoodie. The stress is making me feel frozen, and, despite the heat outside, my hands and feet are like ice.

I feel a hand on my shoulder and look up from my barstool. Uncle Dan looks down at me. "You should play cards with your friends. Keep yourself busy." He sighs.

He still has bare feet, and I stare at them. It's such a simple thing, and yet it tells a glaring story. Uncle Dan is always dressed and ready to go. I don't think I've ever seen him barefoot in my life. He's thrown off and trying to keep his cool just like the rest of us—his bare feet are a telltale sign of his vulnerability and the gravity of the situation.

"Maybe I'll join the next game." I shrug, but I doubt he buys the lie. He takes the stool next to me and puts one of his hands on mine.

"You're a strong girl, Hats, I know that. You don't have to be strong here, though, not with the people that love you."

I narrow my eyes at him. "Would you say the same thing to Danny right now?" I'm deflecting, but I can't help it. If I were a boy, would everyone be so concerned about me?

"Danny?" His eyebrows pull together. "I wouldn't tell Danny that I thought he was strong; I'd have to tell him to chill out. He'd be a nervous wreck right now. He could never hide his feelings as well as you can." He chuckles at his own words.

I smile in spite of myself. He's right—if Danny were here, he'd be yelling at all of us, asking why no one was doing anything and generally just causing as much drama as he could without meaning to. Danny was not the type of person you looked to for guidance in an emergency. He'd have your back one hundred percent, but he would be a mess through all of it.

"I guess you're right. I wish he was here anyway, drama and all."

"Me, too." Uncle Dan smiles, patting my hands and standing. "I'm going to try to call my contact again, see if they've lifted the coms blackout yet."

Communication blackouts are pretty common and don't always mean trouble. Sometimes it's just a security measure. After an attack like this, though, they're necessary to keep soldiers from getting news out before families can be notified of their loss and to keep panic at a minimum. The military needs to control the flow of information. I understand the reasons, but it doesn't suck any less being in the dark and waiting helplessly from thousands of miles away.

Uncle Dan goes to Dad's office to make his call in private, so I pour myself a glass of water and cradle it in my hands. This room is filled with everyone that's important to me, aside from Dad, and, surprisingly, I find their presence calming. I've spent my entire life trying to hold everyone at arm's length so they can't hurt me, so they can't walk away and leave me reeling. Like Mom, and Nana, and now Danny... And yet, this group of people has weaseled their way past my walls and into my heart, and I couldn't be more thankful to have them. Maybe what makes life worth living is having people you don't want to lose.

"Girlfriend!" Sam yells at me. "Get over here. We dealt you some cards, and I need you to kick your boyfriend's butt!"

My cheeks heat—that's the first time someone has referred to Kellan as my boyfriend. We didn't officially name our relationship or anything, and I risk a look his way. He's grinning at me. He puts his hand out to me from the floor, and I take it confidently, sitting between them at the coffee table.

My boyfriend.

Kellan Anderson is my boyfriend.

"Alright, you two," I say confidently, "prepare to be schooled."

———— ♡ ♡ ♡ ————

It's getting late, and the sun has been down for a few hours. We still haven't heard anything, and hope is fading quickly. Uncle Dan has made dozens of phone calls throughout the day, but no one has any new information. I tried to turn on the international news earlier, but Melissa quickly turned that off. Uncle Dan sided with her, saying anything we heard on there would probably be false, anyway, that they wouldn't name anyone before families were notified.

Sam's mom calls first—it's Sunday, and we all are supposed to go to school in the morning. Worrying about missing school seems so trivial when I've barely buried my brother and have no idea what has happened to Dad. Yesterday, I was ready to go back to school—I do understand the importance, but I just feel helpless. Everything is mixed up.

As Sam gathers her things, she nods toward Kellan, who has fallen asleep sitting up on the couch. "You sure you just talked last night? The boy looks beat!" She winks at me.

"Positive, you perv." I laugh, stuffing her purse into her hands. "Thanks for being here today."

"You know I'm always here, Hattie, even when you refuse to ask for my help. Let me know if you need a ride to school in the morning. Though I'm sure everyone will understand if you don't make it just yet." We hug goodbye, and she heads out into the night.

"You have really good friends. I'm glad," Melissa says from the chair. She's changed into weirdly festive pajamas with candy canes printed on them and is sipping tea from a mug.

"I am pretty lucky. I don't make it easy to be my friend." I shrug. I really suck at vulnerability. I get an A for effort when it comes to pushing people away, though.

Melissa nods. "You're like the men in this family. You guard your heart, and that's okay. Sometimes, though, the bravest thing you can do is let people in."

I like her. I haven't spent any time getting to know this woman, and I really should. Especially knowing that Uncle Dan wants to marry her. She could be "Aunt Melissa" soon.

"I am like them, huh?" I ask, the thought warming me. These men—Danny, Dad, Uncle Dan—they're the people who have made me who I am, and I'm proud to be compared to any of them. I carry so many pieces of Danny with me—and of Dad, too.

Uncle Dan moves behind Melissa, putting his hands on her shoulders gently and leaning down to kiss the top of her head. "How are my two favorite girls getting along?" I hear teasing in his voice, but the question feels genuine.

"Just fine, thank you." I laugh, waving him off. He's probably afraid I'm being my stoic teenager self and scaring her away. But it's been such a traumatic few weeks, it's a miracle that any of us can joke at all.

"Should we wake up your... friend?" Uncle Dan asks, shooting a look Kellan's way. He's still asleep, his head propped in his hand. "Something going on there?" He wiggles his eyebrows like Danny used to.

My face instantly heats. "Um... yeah, I think he's my boyfriend."

Uncle Dan's hands clap together, and he actually whoops. "About freakin' time!"

Kellan jerks awake from the commotion. "Huh? What'd I miss?" he asks, wiping his eyes. He looks ruffled and sexy, and I still can't believe he's really mine.

"Nothing, just my crazy uncle being embarrassing." I give him a pointed look, and he pretends to zip his lips. Melissa just chuckles into her mug. These are definitely my people.

"Should you be getting home, son? School tomorrow and all that?" he asks Kellan, and I'm thankful he seems to be done teasing me for a minute.

"We're going to go get ready for bed, Hattie. We'll tuck you in before lights out." Melissa tugs Uncle Dan out of the room, shooting me a wink. I like her more and more by the minute.

Kellan stands up and stretches his arms above his head. His shirt rides up, and I see the briefest flash of his tanned stomach. Butterflies swarm me, and I swallow hard. He's so beautiful.

He's in front of me in three long strides, and his hands cup my jaw. "I can sneak in the window if you want me to stay." He touches his forehead to mine.

"I think maybe we should just try to get some sleep tonight. Hopefully, we will hear something soon. I'll call you right away if we get any news." I wrap my arms around his waist and hold him to me. "But you can drive me to school tomorrow if you want."

"You got it, babe." He smiles, his dimple flashing.

"Babe?" I narrow my eyes.

"Nah? Just trying it out." He laughs.

"I like it, babe." I stretch up on my toes and kiss his soft lips. My heart is hurting, I'm missing Danny, and I'm terrified for Dad, but in Kellan's arms, I get the briefest moments of hope and happiness.

I end our kiss before it gets too heated—I'm almost positive Uncle Dan is right around the corner spying on us. "See you in the morning, Kel. Thanks for everything."

He blushes. "No thanks needed; I'm here whenever you need me." We hug one last time, and then I push him out the front door before I can give in to the desire to drag him back to my room.

No sooner has the door shut behind me than Uncle Dan comes waltzing back into the living room. "So you two are finally a thing, huh?" he asks playfully. "I feel like I should be giving you rules and telling you to keep it PG... but I kinda just want to give you a high five and an attaboy." He does a little dance and throws up a hand for a high five.

I can't help it—I start laughing, and then I can't stop. He looks ridiculous, and he's right—everyone probably knew this was inevitable except for me and Kellan. Denial to the extreme.

I laugh so hard I sit down on the floor, and I can't seem to catch my breath. I laugh because I think I'm in love with the one boy that is supposed to be off-limits. I laugh because I am surrounded by people who want to make everything better for me, who are loving me as hard as I will let them. I laugh because I'm worried about my silly teenage love life when my brother was just buried and my father is missing and possibly dead.

I laugh until the laughing becomes sobbing, painful, body-shaking sobs that release a dam of tears that I've held back for days. I curl my body into a ball and give in to the storm.

Uncle Dan rubs my back and says soothing words as I bleed my feelings onto the floor of the living room.

They refuse to be held back any longer, and now I'm hemorrhaging every emotion my body can contain. He picks me up and carries me to my bed, placing me under the covers fully clothed.

Once I'm tucked into bed, he pats my sobbing, cocooned body and speaks to me softly. "Just let it out, baby girl. Melissa and I are just down the hall if you need us. Don't feel like you have to go to school tomorrow, either; take your time." He shuts off the light, leaving the door ajar. I curl up tighter and let myself come apart.

26

Back to the Grind

AT SOME POINT, MY sobs give way to sleep, and I wake up at 0500 to the school alarm on my phone. Luckily, I remembered to plug my phone in last night before things got crazy.

It's early enough that I have time to shower before I leave. Though I think I'll need all the makeup I own to cover up the evidence of last night's sob fest.

I stand in my bathroom while the water heats and look at my reflection in the mirror. My eyes are slightly red and swollen, but I don't look nearly as bad as I expected. I do look older somehow, though, changed.

I strip naked and let the hot water scald my skin. I feel cried out, which is good—maybe I can make it through one school day without any tears. I wash my hair and imagine all my fear and pain washing down the drain with the suds.

Dad is going to be okay. He has to. Life is cruel, but I have this feeling that things will turn around if I just believe it with all my heart.

Visualize the outcome, Hattie. Believe that it will happen, and take the steps to get there. I use Dad's mantra to propel myself forward.

With my makeup done and my hair dried and curled, I make my way to the kitchen. I shove all the homework I've managed to accomplish into my backpack, but I know I've barely made a dent in the missing assignments. Some of my teachers will likely give me an extension anyway.

Worrying about schoolwork seems so normal.

Melissa is an angel, and she made sure my favorite jeans were ready for me. They were folded on my bed next to a gorgeous green sweater when I got out of the shower.

I find her in the kitchen making tea in her candy cane pajamas. She grabs another mug when she sees me. "Vanilla chai?" she asks softly.

"Perfect, thanks." I reach for a banana and take a stool, and then I send Kellan a text to let him know I'm ready when he is. Melissa finishes making the tea and sets it in front of me. "Thanks for the sweater; it's beautiful," I say.

"Matches your eyes—I thought you'd look pretty in it."

"I guess it does." I hope Uncle Dan does marry this sweet soul.

"You can call us anytime today, and one of us will come get you, no questions asked." She puts a warm hand on mine briefly and then turns back to get her own tea. I appreciate the escape hatch, but I need to do this for my sanity.

"I'll keep my cell on vibrate. Please call me the second you hear anything about Dad." I hear the plea in my own voice. I know they wouldn't make me wait, but I feel the need to voice the request anyway.

Uncle Dan strides into the kitchen then. He's wearing basketball shorts and a plain white undershirt, and he's in desperate need of a shave—it's a funny sight. He goes straight to Melissa, kissing her full on the mouth before turning to me. I love seeing this side of him.

"You're really going to school? Can't persuade you to give it another week?" he asks. I stall, finishing my banana before answering him.

"I can't sit around here waiting to hear about Dad. I need something to keep my brain busy. I totally understand why you're worried... last night, I was a mess." I take a few sips of my tea and choose my words carefully. "But I need to do this, and Kellan and Sam will keep an eye on me. I know you have both of their cell numbers. I'll come straight home after school."

He shakes his head softly. "I'm so proud of you. You inspire me, kid. You're tougher than some of these fully grown men I deal with on a daily basis. Just remember: We are a family, and you're not alone. No matter what, I've got you."

———— ♡ ♡ ♡ ————

Kellan pulls up in his truck, and I hop in before he can come to a complete stop. "Quick, get us out of here before Dan runs out with a plastic lunch box or something." It's foggy and cold this morning, and it looks like rain may start at any moment.

"He's not ready to let you go, huh?" Kellan smiles at me. "I don't blame him. I'm pretty attached, too."

I roll my eyes. "Don't you have football plays to memorize or something?" I cover my mouth with my hand, instantly regretting my comment. *Humor is good for covering up grief, but geez, Hattie, think before you speak.*

Kellan winces a little but recovers quickly. "Coach hasn't really been his normal self. Last week, he came to school in jeans and cowboy boots and sent us out to run without him. He basically gave us the week off from practice. The next game is Friday, but even the second-string quarterback isn't happy to fill Danny's position. We all feel weird playing without him." I notice circles under his eyes and the way his jaw seems tense and rigid. He's trying to hold it together as much as I am.

"I'm sorry, Kellan. I know you miss him, too. Nothing feels right without him." I take his hand in mine while he drives, and we listen to the radio. Both of us are quiet, lost in thoughts and memories of Danny.

We get to school a little early, and the parking lot is mostly empty. The leaves are falling from the trees now and piling up on the sidewalks. A light rain fell last night, so everything is damp, and the rising sun makes the ground seem to sparkle. The big brick school building looks a deeper shade of red when it's wet, and I try to remember if I've noticed that before.

Kellan has been quiet, letting me stare out the window with the music playing low in the background. I'm still holding his hand, his long, strong fingers intertwined with mine. The first bell rings in the distance, and I square my shoulders. Kellan tugs our joined hands to his chest, just over his heart.

"You ready for this, babe?" he says with a smile that doesn't quite reach his eyes.

I release his hand and then my seatbelt, tugging my backpack on over my shoulders. "No, but let's do it." It's now or never.

———— ♡ ♡ ♡ ————

The morning goes by quickly, and my teachers are very understanding. They had a meeting and decided that since I've always been a devoted student, they won't count my missing work against me; I can just pick up where everyone is now. I know they're trying to relieve as much stress as they can, but now they've taken away the distraction of catching up. A distraction I was counting on.

Sam has been calling to check on me between each class, and I've been texting updates to Kellan, too. It keeps me occupied in the downtime.

Soon I have only a few minutes left until lunch, and I'm ready for a break. Everyone has been nice, and I feel like such a jerk for thinking it, but I wish they'd just leave me alone. On a normal day, they would all happily ignore me, and I want that back. I want to blend into the crowd and just get through the day.

There are small shrines to Danny all over the school, just like Sam warned. Candles in various stages of melt, vases of flowers, photos; it's both beautiful and heartbreaking.

No one seems to know the current situation with Dad. Only Sam and Kellan know, and clearly, neither of them has said anything to anyone. Gossip travels at light speed around here, so if a single person knew, I would have heard about it by now. Uncle Dan must have decided not to let the school in on it, either; the teachers are worse than the kids with hot gossip.

The bell rings, and I grab my notebook, making a beeline for my locker. I don't want any of my classmates to ask me how I'm holding up or tell me how sorry they are for my loss right now.

As usual, Sam beats me to my locker. She's wearing black skinny jeans with pink ballet flats and a matching pink sweater. It buttons down the front, and her boobs are threatening to spill out of it at any moment. I envy her confidence sometimes.

"Hey, Hatts!" she says, moving to the side so I can open my locker. "What's the lunch plan today?"

"Cafeteria? I think it's taco salad day." I shrug. I actually love the school's greasy taco salads.

"Is Kellan joining us?" She winks, and I laugh.

"I didn't ask—would that be weird?" I shut my locker and lean back against it next to Sam. We watch the students rushing around the hallways, eager to get to lunch. A few of them turn to give me sympathetic looks as they pass.

Sam shoots daggers at them with her eyes. "He's your man now, right? Not weird at all." I give her a tight hug, and she squeezes me back before linking arms with me. "Let's go find Mr. Hottie right now."

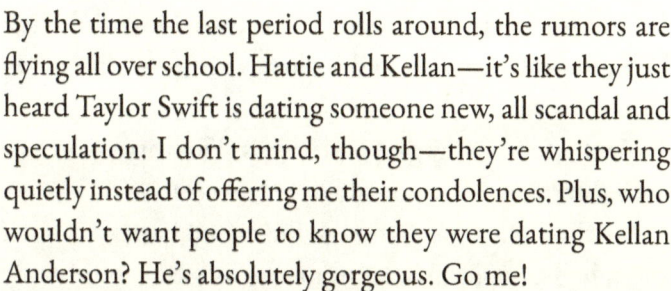

By the time the last period rolls around, the rumors are flying all over school. Hattie and Kellan—it's like they just heard Taylor Swift is dating someone new, all scandal and speculation. I don't mind, though—they're whispering quietly instead of offering me their condolences. Plus, who wouldn't want people to know they were dating Kellan Anderson? He's absolutely gorgeous. Go me!

I start changing into my gym clothes when a familiar voice pipes up. "Hattie, you're back!" Kristin hugs me awkwardly, a wide smile on her freckled face. "Don't put those horrible shorts on—I got you something." Her braid swings back and forth as she digs in her locker. Then she tosses me a folded pair of black yoga pants.

"I got two pairs, and one accidentally came in as a small. I immediately thought it was fate—you were meant to have them. We missed you around here."

"I bet your bestie, Josh, missed me the most." We both laugh. "Thanks a lot, Kristin, this is so nice." She just nods, and we get dressed quietly. She leaves so much unsaid between us, and I appreciate her silence.

A lump forms in my throat. Even with everything that's happened recently, I do have a lot of people that care about me. And thanks to Kristin, I can finally burn those despicable shorts.

I check my phone one last time, but Uncle Dan still hasn't text with any news. I send him a text letting him know I'm in the gym for the next hour and won't have access to my phone. His response is a thumbs-up emoji. I shake my head and hurry out of the locker room.

Kellan is leaning against the wall talking with Josh and some of the other athletes when I emerge from the girls' room. His back is to me, and I admire him while he's unaware—all broad shoulders, lean waist, and strong, tan legs.

Kristin follows my gaze and smirks. "So story is you two are a thing now? I'm pretty jelly! He's a real catch!"

My cheeks flush even though I'm not embarrassed. She's right; he's a total catch, and I'm a lucky girl. I could easily have been friend-zoned given how long we've known each other. "Yes, I guess the rumor mill got it right for once." I wink at her.

"Girl, you're my hero. I knew there was more going on there!" She giggles, and we take our spots on the gym floor.

In a flurry of tight jeans and cowboy boots, Coach prances to the front of the class as the bell rings. I've never seen him in anything but athletic wear, and it throws me off. I stare at him—he even has a strange handlebar-like mustache twisted up at the sides. It's like a weird, evil twin has taken over his body. Or is Coach the evil one, and this is the nice guy? I cover my mouth to keep from laughing out loud.

He seems to notice me in the middle of his instruction, and his voice jumps. He tells everyone to check the whiteboard in the weight room for today's workout and then heads back toward his office. "Tate, my office," he barks over his shoulder.

I shoot a glance at Kellan, but he just shrugs and looks concerned. Coach is definitely not himself. I walk quickly to the office, my Converse squeaking on the polished floor. Better to get this over with quickly. I want to talk to Kellan and calm my nerves.

"Ms. Tate, please have a seat," Coach says, and my jaw falls open at his use of the word "please"—I had decided that the word didn't exist in his vocabulary.

His office is basically a closet. Besides his desk and desk chair, I see only one old crimson chair. The vinyl seat is cracked and worn, and the wooden legs look like a dog chewed on them at some point. He has no decoration on the walls, just piles of paperwork and miscellaneous gym equipment crammed in every corner.

"Is everything okay, Coach?" I ask. Maybe he hit his head or something. I sit in the worn chair and tap my feet on the floor.

"I just wanted to tell you how sorry I am about your brother. I love all my boys like my own children; that's why I'm so tough on them. I like to teach them as much as I can in the short time I have with them. Danny was one of the special ones— he was constantly teaching me new things." His eyes look wet, and I try not to stare at his display of emotion. My own tears well in the corners of my eyes.

"He really loved you, too," I say softly.

"You're a special girl, Henrietta. You don't try as hard as you could in my class, but your teachers and your peers respect you, and I admire that." He takes a breath. "I wanted to ask a favor of you." Coach leans back in his computer chair and seems to search the ceiling for his next words. He crosses and uncrosses his orange snakeskin cowboy boots.

"Thank you, Sir," I say, trying to understand why he's complimenting me.

"I wanted to talk to you about Kellan. He's a promising coach—I know that's what he'd like to do as a career. He's an excellent player, but he's an even better leader. He has a really good way with people. But I'm afraid that losing Danny is going to break him, take away that drive to follow his dream."

"Coach? What does this have to do with me?" I shift uncomfortably in my chair.

"I've heard the rumors, and I've seen the two of you together myself so I know they're true. All I'm asking is that you two lean on each other, ask for help if you need it, even talk to me if it helps. Talk to someone. Things like this have a way of changing people, breaking them. The best thing we can do is stand together."

"Yes, Sir, I will do my best." I mean it, too. I will always be there for Kellan, and I think the same is true in reverse. Though this conversation is awkward, I know Coach is just coming from a place of love.

My head hurts—this has been such a weird day. It feels overwhelming. I just want to dial it back and get through the rest of it.

I want my dad.

I close my eyes and will the Universe to give him back to me. I imagine him in detail, his silvery white hair, the crow's feet around his eyes that crinkle when he laughs—I love his deep, timbral laugh. The eyes that are mirror images of my own: a deep, forest green flecked with gold.

His strong shoulders and scarred hands, the arms that held me only a few days ago. I beg the stars and the moon and the ocean and whatever powerful magical things I can think of to send him back to me safely. I feel tears leak down my cheeks.

Coach coughs quietly. "I didn't mean to upset you. You may rejoin the class if you like."

When I dare to open my eyes, I swear I can see Dad coming through the gym doors.

He's wearing his company shirt with black slacks tucked into black combat boots and tied up tightly. His hair is perfectly spiked as he strides in with the kind of authority that can only be earned through experience. He looks powerful and dangerous, and my heart squeezes hard in my chest. I'm conjuring lifelike images now. I think it's time to call it a day and go home.

Rising from my chair, I step into the gym and freeze. The mirage of my dad has locked eyes with me, and his chest heaves. My breath catches; I can't tear my gaze away.

He closes the distance between us in a flash, and strong arms crush around me tightly. "Oh, Hattie girl, I'm so sorry," he says, his hands rubbing up and down my back, holding me so tightly it almost hurts. But I don't want him to let go. I'm afraid at any moment he'll disappear into thin air, nothing more than a figment of my desperate imagination.

"Dad, are you really here?" My voice comes out small, childlike. I grip fistfuls of his shirt in my hands, pressing my cheek into his chest. He smells like home.

"I'm here, Hattie, and I promise, I'm never leaving you again."

27

Something Broken

TEN MINUTES LATER, I had changed out of my gym clothes, crammed all my things haphazardly into my backpack, and promised to call Sam and Kellan and explain everything later. The look of relief and joy that had flashed across Kellan's face when he saw my dad just made me fall for him even more.

Dad leads me out to his SUV in the visitor parking lot. There are still thirty minutes left in the school day, so we're completely alone out here. A storm is rolling in, and the wind whips across my skin. I shudder from the cold. Dad reaches for me again, hugging me tightly to him. "I love you, Hattie. I'm so sorry that I left."

Part of me still thinks this is all in my imagination, that at any moment, Dad will fade into thin air or I'll wake up from this dream. He's hugging me and telling me things I want to hear, which is so not like us. Except it has been lately, and he feels solid in my arms.

"How are you here?" I ask. I'm glad that he is, but I'm really confused. He's supposed to be halfway across the world, unaccounted for.

"I landed in Germany and checked my voicemail while we taxied. I had three messages. One was from the hospital—they had the autopsy results for Danny, and they wanted me to call back ASAP. The second was from your mother, chewing me out for raising an ungrateful brat." He smiles and winks at me before adding, "And the last one was from Kellan."

Kellan? Why would Kellan call my dad? I want to know all the details, but my brain is stuck on the autopsy results. Dad must know the reason for Danny's death; I can see the pain written on his face.

"What happened, Dad? What did the hospital tell you?" Dad reaches around me and opens the passenger door.

"Let's go home, get warm. I'll tell you everything."

———— ◦ ♡ ◦ ————

A welcoming party greets us when we get home: Uncle Dan, Melissa, and a few of Dad's veteran friends that live nearby. The news that he's returned home has traveled quickly. Apparently, he called when he landed in Killeen but had asked Uncle Dan not to let me know—he figured I'd take the news better in person. When I got the thumbs-up emoji in gym class, Uncle Dan was talking to Dad on the phone and letting him know where he could find me.

All these big, strong men have even bigger emotions. They take turns hugging Dad in that manly way, clapping each other hard on the back. There are a lot of "hooah"s exchanged and smiles all around. One of their own has lived to fight another day, and they know how important it is to celebrate these things.

I let Dad have his moment, excusing myself to my own room. I stash my backpack, take off my shoes, and wash my face. I stare at my own reflection in the bathroom mirror. I look like I've been through hell, but I guess, in a way, that is where I've been. I turn my face toward the ceiling and silently thank the powers that be for sending Dad home to me. Maybe they had nothing to do with it at all, but it doesn't hurt to cover all the bases.

After I dry my face and shut off the bathroom light, I open the adjoining door to Danny's room, the place that has become my refuge lately. Hazy light filters through the window and gives his walls a warm glow despite the storm. I sit on the edge of his bed and take a deep breath; his smell still lingers all around.

"God, Danny, I really miss you," I say aloud. I still don't feel him like everyone else claims they can, but I hope he can hear me wherever he is now. "Dad's back, but I'm sure you already know that. I don't know how, but I'm damn grateful. Losing you was bad enough—I am not ready to be the sole survivor over here. Keep an eye on him for me, will you?"

I drop back into the comfort of his bed and stare at the ceiling—a few leftover glow-in-the-dark stars are still stuck up there. Evidence of our lives together emanates from every nook and cranny of this house. I hope Dad keeps this house forever. I never realized quite how lucky we were when we stopped moving around. The memories we have here are solid and tangible. They can be felt, held, touched, smelled. I close my eyes and conjure up as many memories as I can.

"Hattie?" Dad calls softly, and I open my eyes and sit up. He's standing in the bathroom doorway watching me. I don't think he's been in Danny's room yet, and he seems frozen where he stands. His eyes are sad, and his face is pale. I was lucky enough to be distracted by Kellan that first time.

"Come in, Dad." Dad always responds better to orders than suggestions. "Come sit with me."

He nods and walks slowly to the bed, sitting down beside me. "It looks just like he left it. I keep expecting him to burst through the door and tell us to get the hell out." Dad smiles at the thought. I look around the room; everything is exactly where it belongs, not a dust bunny or sticky fingerprint to be found. Books and movies are perfectly organized and lined up. Even his trash can is perfectly centered against his desk.

"It's definitely cleaner than mine." I shrug. "And he'd probably kill me for going through his things."

"You've been in his closet a lot, or so I hear..." Dad's eyes shoot questions at me. "Find anything worth sharing?" He still has his boots on, and he looks tired and worn.

I wonder if this is the right time to tell him about the journals, but I know he has plenty to tell me, too. "Some. I'll show you sometime," I say instead. "How'd you get back so quick, Dad?"

"Remember I said I had those voicemails?"

"The one from the hospital, the one from Mom complimenting you on your parenting, and the one from Kellan," I answer, hugging my knees to my chest, eager to hear more.

"Your mother is who she is. Try not to let her get to you, Hattie. She wanted some things from me, and she's not getting them. I'm sorry that she thought going through you would make me change my mind. If I'd known she was going to show up in town, I would have warned you." He presses his lips together and then takes a deep breath.

"What things does she want?"

"Money. She knows that there is a life insurance policy for your brother, and she wanted half of it. I wasn't going to tell you this, but it doesn't feel right to keep it from you, either." His shoulders slump a little, and I lean into him.

"I think she's sick," I say, and I really mean it. "She needs some serious mental help. She's like a real-life evil stepmother, minus the whole 'step' part."

Dad chuckles and squeezes an arm around my shoulders. "I'm glad you still have your sense of humor. You've always been a special kid. Don't lose that fire, Hattie."

I shake my head. "Is there no limit to the nerve of that woman?"

"I don't regret marrying your mother; she gave me the two of you, after all." Dad winks, but I feel like he's letting her off easy. I'd say so, but I have a more pressing agenda. I want answers.

"Okay, so that explains the *Mom*-ster, but what did Kellan call you for?" I'm a little afraid to hear the answer to this one. I can't think of a single reason Kellan would have to call my dad.

Rubbing his hand up and down my arm, Dad says quietly, "He wanted me to know that he was looking out for you while I was on assignment. That we would always be part of his family, and that's what family does. I have to be honest—it really hit me hard."

Tears have already started falling down my face. At this point, I should just resign myself to a lifetime of crying my eyes out. Grief or not, I'm a leaky faucet. Maybe I'm making up for all of the years I never cried.

Kellan really is amazing, the definition of valiant and honorable. He'd done such a touching thing without being asked or expecting anything in return. My heart swells in my chest as I think of him leaving that message for Dad.

"About Kellan... we're kind of seeing each other." I figure it's best to just be honest and upfront about this now. No sense trying to hide it—for all I know, Uncle Dan already spilled the beans about us, anyway.

Dad lets out a long breath, his arm around me tightening just a little. "I knew this day would come. I think he's a good choice, Hattie, and I trust you with your own private relationships. I'm here if you ever want advice or anything, but I won't pry. It's not my style."

This time, it's me that chuckles. "Since when?"

Dad laughs at that, too, and we share a knowing look. "Okay, okay, message received. I'll try not to dictate or control the situation. That's the best I can do."

"I appreciate the willingness to try." I smirk back at him, punching him playfully in the chest before changing the subject. "You said something in the gym today about never leaving me again. Did you mean it?" I'm stalling. I want to know what happened to Danny, but I'm afraid it'll feel so final.

Dad shifts on the bed, his jaw set. "It's time to step down. I can still own this company and let some of the younger, more eager guys lead the fight. I don't have to be the one over there sorting through operations. I have excellently trained men working for me; it's about time I let them use the skills I hired them for."

"You're quitting?" The words fly out of my mouth, and my eyes widen as I find his gaze.

"Not quitting—I don't see it that way. There is a difference between quitting and knowing when you've had enough. I'm needed here now. It's time to step back and reevaluate my priorities. There's nothing more important to me than spending time with you now."

What a curveball. Never in a million years would I have imagined those words coming from my dad. My body buzzes with a swirling mess of emotions as Dad pulls me closer. He won't be in danger anymore, but he can still do his job, and we can be a real family. I wish, not for the first time, that Danny was here for this.

I sense a strange, peaceful feeling spreading throughout my body. I've spent my entire life wondering if Dad's next trip would take his life. I feel as though a huge weight has been lifted off my shoulders knowing that this chapter has closed.

We still have one more heavy topic to discuss, though, and I try to hold on to the happiness in my heart as I ask, "And the hospital?"

Letting go of my shoulders, Dad turns toward me, his face growing serious. "Hattie, when I called the hospital back, they were really concerned."

With those words, I am on full alert, suddenly hyperaware of his every move.

"Your brother had an undiagnosed heart defect. A congenital heart defect that somehow went unnoticed from birth. Apparently, that happens a lot, though less often now that they have better technology for screening during pregnancy. But it still happens. Turns out, one out of every one hundred children is born with some kind of heart defect. I had no idea." Dad scrubs his face with his hands, taking his time to sort out his thoughts.

"They believe his heart defect—paired with his heavy athletic training and the stress from the game—triggered his sudden cardiac arrest. They're not entirely in agreement on which specific defect he had, but it could certainly be genetic, and they'd like to get an echocardiogram done on your heart just to be safe. I've made an appointment in Temple for tomorrow—I don't want to wait another day without knowing for sure. I cannot risk losing another child." Dad's body shakes, and he begins to cry.

My brain feels frozen, on a loop.

Heart defect.

His heart was broken.

His broken heart took his life and left all of ours shattered in its wake.

We are all just a mess of bleeding hearts now. Crimson hearts.

I keep seeing him on the ground, his eyes closed, his body too still. If we had known sooner, would he still be here with us? Could all of this heartache have been avoided? I remember he seemed extra tired during the last few days before he died, but I thought it was just from practicing so hard and stressing about the big game. All that extra physical activity over the summer—could that have been what triggered this? My mind spins.

I know the "what if" game is a dangerous one to play, but it's hard not to go there. I don't even let myself think about what it could mean if I have the same problem.

One thing at a time.

Shaking myself free of my heavy thoughts, I dry my tears with my shirt sleeve. I pull Dad into a hug and take comfort in his arms. He kisses the top of my head, so I close my eyes, savoring this moment. The only thing missing here is Danny.

"It'll all work out," I tell him, and, surprisingly, I think I actually believe it.

28

Crimson Hearts

THE WAITING ROOM AT the Pediatric Cardiologist's office in Temple is mostly empty, and I fidget in my too-small seat. I feel funny seeing a kid doctor when I'm almost an adult—this entire hospital is dedicated to children's care. The furniture is all made to look like crayons and Legos, and Dad looks hilarious sitting in one of the chairs. I would probably be laughing and teasing him about it if I didn't feel so nervous. As it is, I'm using all my concentration not to regurgitate my breakfast.

The receptionist at the desk keeps looking over at us and smiling sympathetically. I wonder if she even knows she's doing it. She has a Winnie the Pooh print on her scrubs, and even her nails have little cartoon characters on them. I feel out of place here—between me pumping my leg up and down, and Dad sitting ramrod straight, looking ready to attack, she probably thinks we're about to lose it. Who knows; maybe we are.

"Henrietta Tate?" a nurse calls out, and I jump out of my skin.

"Would you like me to come with you?" Dad asks, and I nod. I'm terrified, and I don't want to do this alone. Maybe I do belong in the pediatric office.

———— ♡ ♡ ♡ ————

The cardiologist, who is overly animated and has asked us to call him "Dr. John," has been performing the echocardiogram on my heart for almost thirty minutes now. He's using what's basically an ultrasound machine, and he's been busily clicking away for several minutes now.

I'm lying flat on the bed on my back in my jeans and a sports bra. There are posters of puppies and kittens taped to the ceiling tiles. Dr. John put some weird gel in a pile on my chest, and now it's been smeared everywhere from his wand.

The room is small, and we all barely fit in here. Dad is waiting on the other side of a privacy curtain since I'm half naked, but I'm glad that they allowed him to stay.

The doctor told us before starting that he would be quiet during the process and tell us the results afterward, which felt more like a warning than anything else. I have been watching the screen, but I don't know what any of the flashing colors mean. Each time he moves the wand, I see another view of the heart. Red and blue lights flash in what I can only assume are valves and chambers. I wish I'd paid more attention in anatomy class. Occasionally, I see him type in a description, but other than that, the images are useless to me. I keep glancing at the clock on the wall and wondering if it's taking too long, wondering if that might be a bad sign.

Dad has been talking to me quietly the entire time. To the untrained ear, Dad sounds calm and collected, the picture of patience. But I can hear the hitch in his voice, the strain in his jaw. He's worried, and it makes me feel less alone.

There are pictures of impossibly tiny babies, smiling toddlers, and kids of every age all the way up to almost adults in the hallway. They all have long, red scars on their chests, which they display proudly in the photos, and the captions read things like "Heart Warrior" and "Heart Angel." I guess that means Danny is technically a Heart Angel now. I have a feeling he would love that.

Dr. John turns on his stool. "Take a moment to get cleaned up, Ms. Hattie, and then meet your father and me in the office across the hall." They leave me alone in the room. I'm terrified and feel the nausea return with a vengeance. I clean the gel mess off with a towel and pull my shirt over my head as quickly as my shaking hands will allow.

Dad and Dr. John are sitting silently at a round table in the office. Medical books sit in piles on the floor and fill up two large bookshelves. Otherwise, this room is empty. One entire wall is a window, and the light feels too bright for my eyes. I take a seat next to Dad, and he reaches out to hold one of my hands in his. I return his squeeze.

"Well, friends, today I get to say something I don't often get to say around here." He places both of his hands flat on the table.

"What's that?" I ask, my voice shaking.

"You have a boring, healthy, normal heart!" He chuckles and claps his hands together. "I'd still recommend that when you have children of your own, you get extra pictures of their hearts taken during pregnancy because these things can run in families. But, Ms. Tate, I'm happy to say you are heart healthy."

———— ♡ ♥ ♡ ————

The drive home from Temple takes a little over an hour. I'm dying to get home and call Sam and Kellan—I would do it now, but I feel like I want a little time to process everything myself. Dad said I can invite them over for dinner, though, to celebrate the good news. This news just feels like it should be shared in person.

We're both quiet for most of the drive. I feel like finding out my heart isn't a secret landmine has removed the dark cloud over our heads, and now we're just relishing the calm.

Country music plays softly through the speakers, and I stare out the window into the trees. I love central Texas. Of all the places we've lived, this is my favorite. It's slower here, and it's beautiful, especially once the bluebonnets start to bloom everywhere. Besides, for the rest of my life, this will be the place that reminds me the most of Danny. We've done most of our growing up here, side by side.

I can't help but feel guilty that I'm fine and Danny isn't. It's such a strange thing, knowing his heart was struggling all that time. Dr. John assured us that in a lot of cases, the patient has no noticeable symptoms. Danny might have felt extra tired or dizzy in the moments before he died, but he wasn't in massive pain. His assurances don't really make me feel any better about the whole situation, but I am glad Danny didn't suffer.

I wish we could have found out in time to save him, though. I wish for a lot of things. But the important thing now is to honor his memory—he lives on through me and Dad, through Kellan, through everyone else who loved him.

We pull into the driveway, and I notice Kellan's truck and Sam's car parked on our street. Dad smiles at me. "I told Dan if they showed up just to let them in. You have good friends, Hattie. It's clear how much they love you."

I smile back at Dad. He's right about them.

Before he even turns off the car, I'm sprinting up the driveway to the front door. It flies open before I get there, and Kellan runs out of the house to meet me.

"I'm okay!" I cry out, a grin spreading across my face.

He slams into me halfway down the sidewalk, scooping me off my feet in his arms and twirling me around in a circle before planting a kiss on my lips. "Thank God." He sighs, setting me down and touching his forehead to mine.

"Get out of my way, and let me hug my friend, loverboy." Sam squeals, pushing Kellan away from me. She hugs me tightly, her wild red curls flying into both of our faces. "Girl, we've been going crazy waiting for you." I hear tears in her voice.

"I knew my heart would be okay—you'd kill me otherwise," I joke.

"Damn straight, I would!"

I nudge her playfully. "Dad wants to feed you both dinner, so let's get inside and order everything."

Sam laughs long and hard. "Now you're speaking my language."

Following them into the house, I see everyone I love has gathered into our small living room. Dad, Uncle Dan, Melissa, Sam, Kellan—even a few of Dad's stragglers are smiling at me. Dad is talking softly to Uncle Dan, and I see a new light in him. Maybe knowing he doesn't have to go back to a warzone again has already started to change him. I really hope so.

The room is warm, the mood light. Everyone is talking and joking around, and I stand in the entryway and take it all in. I feel cherished and loved in this moment.

I close my eyes and think of Danny. "I think we'll be okay," I say to him softly.

The strangest sensation comes over me. With my eyes still closed, I feel Danny's arms wrap around me from behind, just like he used to do. The weight of him is almost too much for my short legs to bear. I can smell the same cinnamon and spice scent from his room—it swirls around me.

"You'll be more than okay, punk. You're a Tate." I hear his voice chuckle, and then, just like that, he's gone.

Epilogue

MAY

Dear Danny,

It's been almost eight months since you left us. We're still getting used to life without you. I don't think we'll ever completely get used to it, and I'm okay with that.

Dad is transitioning pretty well to his new role in his company. But it's really weird to find him home cooking in the kitchen when I get home from work.

Oh, yeah—I got a job! I am working at the old movie theater they converted into a bookstore, All Booked! It's the perfect job for a bookworm like me, and I get a 30% employee discount!

I'm driving your car now. Since I'm working, I need reliable transportation. I promise I'm keeping it cleaner than my room. The job pays for gas and the occasional nights out with Kellan and Sam, but not much more. Dad said he just wants me to have a little work experience before I leave for college.

School gets out for the summer next week—I can't believe graduation is finally here! I get to accept your diploma and *mine at the same time. You know I'll be imagining you up there with us. Kellan is taking it extra hard that you won't be there; stay close to him—he misses you a lot.*

Yes, we're still dating. He's really good to me, Danny. I don't think I could ask for a sweeter boyfriend. Don't roll your eyes, either—I saw what you wrote about him. You should have seen his face when I finally showed him the parts you wrote about being okay with us dating. You two really did have some kind of epic bromance. Definitely Teen Wolf *worthy. He's the Stiles to your Derek.*

Speaking of... I finished watching Teen Wolf. *You would have hated the way they ended it, but I like to think you were watching it with me.*

Kellan is headed to college in the fall—he got into a coach mentoring program at Baylor in Waco. Which is funny, because I just accepted a full-ride scholarship to Baylor as well! Sic 'em, Bears! Dad is just happy I can come home every weekend and he can drop in on me any time he wants.

Turns out, I have a knack for writing about my hero of a twin brother and how much he shaped my life. So I guess you helped me get into college, after all.

Sam is dating a couple of guys right now—she's really embracing the "last year of high school" feeling. She said she doesn't want to be like me and Kellan, starting our college journey tied to a high school relationship. Kellan told her she's just jealous—yeah, the two of them together is a real comedy show.

Dad and I have been seeing a therapist, and we are working on dealing with our grief. Losing you really messed with every part of our lives. We tried for a little while to lean on each other, but we realized we needed something more.

Kellan probably explained it better than anyone. (He's seeing someone, too.) He said: "When you break an arm or a leg, there's a standard healing process. The doctors set the break, immobilize it to keep it from further injury—usually with a cast—and the bone stays protected so that it can heal. In a year or two, you might not even be able to tell on an x-ray that it was ever broken at all.

"When you lose someone close to you, however, and essentially 'break your heart,' there's no set healing process. You can't wrap up your heart and keep it from further injury. You can't check x-rays and watch the healing process. No matter how long it takes, it'll never completely heal. Tiny cracks will always remain, and sometimes they'll feel like gaping holes. The problem with a broken heart is you are on your own."

Guess you're not the only poet around here.

So we lean on each other where we can, and we talk about you all the time. We don't shy away from the tough feelings; we welcome them. The pain we feel is a reminder of the love that we still have for you.

We will always love you.

We're spreading awareness for heart defects now, raising money for research and shouting out your story to anyone who will listen. Coach retired your number, and your old jersey was framed in glass and hangs above the gym scoreboard. I love seeing "TATE" up there in big letters. You deserve it.

Dad started a scholarship fund in your memory for young athletes called the "Crimson Hearts Scholarship." Next year, we will choose the first recipient of the award. You did say you'd always be a Crimson Wolf—I think we all have Crimson Hearts now.

I'm going to keep this journal. I never saw myself as the journaling type, but writing to you feels right. Your journals still get me through the toughest of grief days.

I love you, jerkface.

Always,

Hattie XOXO

Author's Note

Our daughter, Kinley Eleanor, was born on March 9, 2015. She came into this world looking perfectly beautiful and healthy, but we already knew the truth. Her heart was very sick, and she would need open heart surgery within the first week of her life. Kinley had multiple heart defects, Transposition of the Great Arteries (TGA), Coarctation of the Aorta (COA), Ventricular Septal Defect (VSD), and Atrial Septal Defect (ASD). We don't have a prior family history of birth defects, nor was the pregnancy an unhealthy one. I remember the cardiologist telling us that it was like a lightning strike, a random fluke during the development of the heart. Congenital Heart Defects (CHDs) are the most common type of birth defect in the United States, affecting nearly 1% (about 40,000) births per year. CHDs are present at birth, and they affect the structure of a baby's heart and the way it works. About 1 in 4 babies born with a heart defect have a critical CHD and will require surgery or other procedures in their first year of life.

Kinley had open heart surgery on March 16th, 2015, at just a week old. Her surgery was long and difficult and not without unexpected setbacks. She had multiple procedures over the next few days, the surgeons cleaning out blood clots and doing everything they could to keep her stable. Unfortunately, on the morning of March 21st, 2015, at just twelve days old, Kinley lost her battle with CHD.

Our family will never be the same, and there is a Kinley-shaped hole in our lives. While Crimson Hearts is not her story, I wanted to write something that would give you a picture of that grief and make my girl proud. Thank you for reading. If you would like to learn more about Congenital Heart Defects, I encourage you to check out The Children's Heart Foundation website.

Acknowledgments

A special thank you to my husband, Josh, and my four beautiful children. At the end of the day, you are what it's all about. Thank you for supporting me, even when I am off in my own worlds. I love you.

To Kayla Grosse, who spent countless hours in virtual writing dates with me and who helped me make important changes to Hattie's story. The brave face you put on your own heart battle is inspiring—you're an amazing woman and a great friend.

To Nina Wills and her beautiful heart warrior, Peyton, thank you for being there for me when I needed a heart mom to hold my hand. Even though we found out about our heart babies at the same time, you led the way for me, and I am forever thankful for your kindness. I feel so lucky to know you and Peyton. Heart kids are really something special and so are heart moms. Thank you for all of the heart-related content advice and for believing in this book from the very beginning. Give 'em hell, Peyton!

To Sarah Mello, who welcomed me into the self-publishing world with open arms and helped me whip this book into something even more special. You are an amazing woman and a phenomenal writer, and I am so lucky to know you! Thanks for being the best critique partner ever.

To my Bookstagram beta readers: Heidi, Jennifer, Dara, Kaitlyn, Sabrina, Emily, Nina, Danielle G, Megan, and everyone else who read my book and gave me feedback or support, you guys rock! I cannot thank you enough.

To my editor, Melissa Frey, thank you for taking my words and polishing them until they shined and for being the best cheerleader a writer could ask for. You are amazing.

And finally, to my readers! Thank you for supporting me, for loving the characters as much as I do, and for taking a chance on a new author. I am so excited to be on this journey with you.

XOXO
- Nic

Also by Nicole Reeves

What Remains
a gripping tale of survival, self-discovery, love,
and the indomitable human spirit in the face of an
apocalyptic world.

Find Nicole Reeves:

TikTok: @authornicolereeves
Instagram: @nic_reeves_writes

Author Page:
www.nicolereeves.com